A WINDING TRAIL TO JUSTICE

Reluctant Redemption Book 2

REG QUIST

A Winding Trail to Justice
by Reg Quist

Paperback Edition

CKN Christian Publishing
An Imprint of Wolfpack Publishing

6032 Wheat Penny Avenue
Las Vegas, NV 89122

Paperback ISBN: 978-1-64734-312-5
Ebook ISBN: 978-1-64734-311-8
Library of Congress Control Number: 2020935710

A WINDING TRAIL
TO JUSTICE

To the faithful readers who keep me writing.

CHAPTER ONE

Las Vegas, NM

The rattle of gunshots startled Zac out of his half-asleep comfort. Nestled warmly into his favorite chair, in the flickering glow of the big stone fireplace, he was in no mood to move or be bothered.

The day had been long, cold and wet. Now warm after pulling on dry clothing, he had eased into his mohair chair. He was hoping to not be disturbed.

Zac wasn't really a cattleman. He kept just a few head to hold the grass down around the place. He didn't need the money cattle would bring. And he didn't want the work that would go with the care of a larger herd of the brutes. But that didn't mean he favored losing any.

A range-wise old cow took to the brush sometime after lunch to hide her newborn calf. But that meant the calf would also be at the mercy of the many predators that ranged the territory. With the thousands of unused acres of mountainside brush and rock behind the ranch, if he didn't keep track of his animals, they could be miles away in just no time at all. Or dead. Neither thought left him with any good feelings.

After two hours of wet searching, Zac found the pair in a small grove of desert brush and drove them home. By that time, he was thorn scratched, saddle weary and thoroughly done with the miserable, contrary beasts.

Now, with evening coming on and with a pine-log fire roaring close by, Zac had taken to his chair, contentedly resting his feet on a turned-over ammunition box. Such slight comforts come altogether too seldom in rough country.

There was a book lying on his lap, closed, but with a single finger holding the pages apart, marking where he had finished reading. It was getting too dark to read anyway, and in order to light a lamp Zac would have to stand up. But why move when he didn't really have to?

Instead of lighting the lamp, he had allowed himself to drop into a hazy dreamworld. He was hungry and longing for a cup of coffee but was too far into his warming comfort to get up and do for himself.

The word 'cozy' sounded a bit feminine in Zac's thinking. It was unlikely he would have used the word in normal conversation. There was just nothing at all feminine or really, even gentle, in Zac. Still, in the silence of his own mind he thought the word. Cozy.

The first shot shattered his coziness. With the second shot the book flew from his hands, falling to the floor.

The next shot, barely a second after the last one, had him on his knees, hunkered behind his big overstuffed, wing-back chair, with his ever-present Henry pointed towards the kitchen door.

The first thought out of his dazed, half-asleep mind was, the enemy, they're upon us! The war was long past, but it was in no way over for Zac.

It was the familiar feel of the big chair, with his elbow resting on an upholstered arm as it held the Henry, along with the gradual awareness that he was safe in his own ranch house, that slowly dragged the old warrior back from that long-ago war. And from his drowsiness.

Three more shots convinced Zac that none of the lead had been directed his way. And now that he was fully awake, he could tell by the rain and wind-filtered sounds that the shooters were some little ways from the adobe, perhaps out on the town trail.

If there had been shouting or other yahooing to accompany the gun fire, he might have thought it was just a few of the boys celebrating pay day. But there were no Rebel yells and no loud laughter. It wasn't the kind of evening for it anyway.

In any case, his small ranch was all of six miles from Las Vegas, on a winding and uphill trail. It was unlikely any drunks would ride that far or come his way. Even if the wind and rain and threatening, late-spring snow didn't keep the boys in town, Zac's reputation would surely turn them in another direction.

That's all the time assuming they knew about him and where his ranch lay.

Getting back onto his feet he crouch-walked his way to the side door and carefully stepped into the yard. His woolen, black and white checkered shirt was soaked through in seconds. His long black hair flattened out, wet and limp, clinging to his neck and hanging over his shirt collar.

For the second time that day Zac was thinking evil thoughts about New Mexico's ever changeable weather.

Once in the yard, he almost immediately stepped on a pebble, which his stocking feet offered no protection against.

Ignoring both the pain and the wet, as best he could, he continued his hunched over walk down the side of the adobe ranch house. Very carefully, with the Henry leading the way, he peeked around the front corner and across the patio. There was no one in the yard that he could see.

A new round of firing from outside the ranch gate, about fifty yards away, eased his immediate concern. The dullness of the day and the bend in the trail might be preventing the shooters from seeing the gate, or the darkened ranch itself.

Rising to a full upright position, he took a careful study of everything he could see in the gloomy twilight.

The rain-slick roof of the barn reflected just a slight bit of the last of the day. There had been no actual sunlight since the evening before, just a filtered leakage the dark grey clouds were unable to hold back.

The small adobe that had been a bunkhouse in times past, and that now housed the Gonzales family, or at least all that was left of them, was in darkness, the shutters closed.

Zac hadn't yet lit the lantern that hung over the barn door. Normally he would have seen to that small chore before this hour, but he had opted for the warm fire and somehow, never got the task done.

The yard was dark and empty. But outside the gate there was a shuffling and stamping of horse hooves, at least three or four men laughing and, if his ears weren't still asleep, a woman's mostly stifled scream.

Three more shots blotted out the other sounds. The muzzle flashes told Zac that all the shots were simply pointed into the air, indicating a drunken celebration of some sort.

Taking a last, careful look around his small ranch yard and seeing no threat, Zac started to run. His feet picked up more pebbles and a couple of thorns. He ignored the pain and kept running. He dropped to one knee behind the big gate post that supported the sign announcing the entrance to the Wayward Ranch.

There were no more shots, but he could still hear periodic laughter down the lane a short way. Running in that direction, his sock feet made just a slight sucking noise as they were put down and then pulled from the mud. It wasn't noise enough to alert the shooters.

In just a few seconds he covered the distance to where the revelers were laughing and shuffling their horses in circles, seemingly ignoring the rain.

Zac was within easy shouting distance of the men when he again heard a woman's garbled scream. It was the sound a person might make if someone was holding his hand over her mouth. He was just barely able to make out shapes in the faded light of the rain-soaked evening.

Two mounted men seemed to be totally distracted, laughing and encouraging their friend, who was on foot, holding a struggling woman. With one arm around her waist and the other hand over her mouth, the man said, "Stop the struggling lady or it'll go all the worse for you."

Zac eased ahead, dropping to one knee, close enough to easily see the bunch now. Two men were mounted, their animals circling the man and woman on the ground.

The woman was fighting back with grim determination. She must have bitten her attacker's fingers. He pulled his hand back, crying out in pain before slapping her face with a work-toughened hand. She sagged under the onslaught.

Soon rallying, the woman twisted away from the man as far as she could. She then stepped back before kicking out, connecting a hard-soled riding boot against her attacker's shin. Again, the man cried out, stifling a curse.

Holding her by a twist in the top of her rain jacket, he pulled his other hand back, as if to strike again, this time with a closed fist, when Zac's voice cut through the wet, cold, night air.

"Stand down. All of you. Let the lady go. Do it now."

The response was not what he had hoped for. The man on the ground immediately whirled the woman around, placing her as a shield between Zac and himself. The two men on horseback, lacking sober judgement and ignoring the fact that they were outlined against the cloud darkened sky, pulled their horses up and started lifting their Colts, looking through the rain-soaked gloom for a target. One rider got a single stray shot off, more or less in Zac's direction.

Zac responded in the only way he knew when faced with men holding weapons. He had long experience firing the Henry from hip level. At close range he rarely missed his target. Zac's first shot took one of the revelers in the upper arm, breaking bone and tearing flesh. The man cried out in pain, grabbed his shoulder, lost his balance and toppled into the mud.

Zac's next shot was a clear miss as the rider was swinging his mount in a circle, looking for either a target or for escape. Instead of hitting the assailant directly, Zac's .44 slug ricocheted off the top of his saddle horn. The now deformed chunk of lead slammed into his Colt, blasting it from his hand and tearing off his trigger finger. The shooter's scream of pain was stifled as he fell from the horse. The frantic gelding dragged him fifty feet through the sloppy mud before his foot pulled loose of the stirrup.

As the second shooter fell, the captive woman bent her knees, dropping to the ground, and freeing herself of the distracted attacker's grip.

The now exposed bully immediately raised his arms and shouted out, "No, no, don't shoot. We was just having some fun. Don't shoot."

Zac spoke to the woman.

"If you can stand by yourself, come over here."

"I'm fine," she answered, somewhat belligerently, as she rose to her feet.

She took a single step before whirling towards her attacker. With a doubled fist she struck with all the strength left in her weary body. The blow wouldn't've won a prize fight, but it did mash the attacker's lips and break his nose. A gush of blood poured over his mouth and chin as he stifled a startled cry.

With a half dozen careful steps through the mud she was standing beside Zac, but still out of his reach. Clearly, she didn't yet know if Zac was a man to be trusted or not.

Another voice came out of the dark.

"Is it finished now, Mister Zac?"

The voice belonged to Amado Gonzales. The young man was holding his .22 ca. varmint rifle on the last man standing.

"It's finished Amado. I'd like it if you would take the lady to your Mother. She can get her dried off and perhaps find something for her to wear. Then you come back out here. Leave the house for the women. See if you can get a hand on those loose horses."

The woman cut in with, "I have a horse out there somewhere. Has a pack with a change of clothing in it tied behind the saddle. There's no telling where the beast ran off to."

Zac didn't figure that information was of any particular interest right at the moment. He turned to the man who still had his arms in the air.

"You help your two friends to their feet and walk them through that gate. Just off to the left there's a barn. Head that way. You take one step in any other direction and you'll be dead in the mud."

Zac called out to Amado and the woman, who were ten paces ahead of him.

"Amado. I'd like it if you could light that lantern over the barn door after you get the lady to where it's dry. We'll stand out here until you get it done."

"Si, Mister Zac."

With the window shutters closed on the small house, Zac didn't see a light until Amado opened the door to the adobe.

Mrs. Gonzales took a quick look at the soaked and bedraggled woman who was lamp-lit outside the now open door. With a gasp she tucked her folded hands under her chin. But only for a brief moment.

"Como en. Como en. Oh, you poor lady. Look at you. So wet. So muddy. You must be cold. Como en. We get you to the fire. I make hot coffee. Amado, you go to the barn. Leave us. Oh, poor lady!"

Amado picked a match from the box sitting on top of the stove's warming-oven and went back into the rain, sheltering the match in his cupped hand. He lifted the lantern down and opened the barn door. Inside the small building, sheltered from the wind and rain, he struck the match. The wick had taken on some moisture from the damp air but before the match burned itself out, the kerosene flared to life. Closing the globe, he stepped back outside and hung the lantern above the door.

Swinging one of the double doors wide, he called to Zac.

Within seconds Zac pushed the terrified bully into the barn. His two wounded friends stumbled along beside him. Several horses turned their heads at the scuffling of feet on the straw runway. The milk cow rose to her feet at the disturbance. Her calf immediately took advantage of the unexpected opportunity for a meal.

Zac gave his prisoner another push, this time into an empty stall next to the cow.

"Turn around. Put your hands behind you. Back up to that post. Sit down."

Without taking his eyes off the prisoner Zac spoke to Amado.

"Check those other two for weapons. Pull off their boots. Look for hideout guns."

Thinking that anything was better than lying wounded in the rain and mud, or on the barn floor, the way his two buddies were, the bully did as he was told. Zac took a turn around one wrist with a piece of light rope, pulled the wrist behind the wooden roof support and firmly tied the other hand. He then took a double turn around the man's chest and the post and pulled the rope tight. He knew enough about knots that he was confident the man would be there in the morning.

"I have checked carefully Mister Zac. These man's, they have no more weapons. Two knives I have found. I think so, their guns are lying in the mud."

"Thank you, Amado. Perhaps you could see if your mother can find some bandages. I'll tie up those wounds just as soon as this fella is secure."

Without a word, the young man ran to the house. Within a few minutes he was back. His mother was walking beside him, draped in a heavy woolen poncho. She held a knit, woolen scarf over her head. In her arms, protected from the downpour by the poncho, were some clean cloths and a small metal tub of some mysterious ointment that she placed great faith in.

Mrs. Gonzales sized up the situation in a glance. She pushed Zac out of the way and went to work. With no more than a bit of ointment to stop the infection and a bundle of dry rags to staunch the bleeding, she did what she could.

She looked each suffering man in the eye and then turned to Zac.

"They need doctor."

With that she wrapped the woolen scarf around her head again and left the barn.

Zac was watching the impromptu nurse disappear in the darkness when Amado appeared in the barn doorway, leading the three horses. Another animal, this one loaded down with a bundle tied behind the saddle, followed along without being led.

"Good work, Amado. That fourth one must be the lady's animal." He pointed at the horse with the pack behind the saddle.

"Perhaps you could strip the gear and put him in the stall with that young gelding. They should get along alright."

Amado led the animal with the pack into the barn and lifted off the saddle and the tied-down bundle. Without being asked, he untied the pack.

"I'll take this over to the house."

He was back within a couple of minutes.

"The pretty lady is muy happy to have her things. But the pack, she is demasiado wet. I think so, she will need the clothing to dry beside the stove before she can wear it. Mama has found enough for now."

Zac nodded silently.

CHAPTER TWO

An hour later, with Zac and Amado both in dry clothes again, with cups of strong coffee Zac had finally worked up the energy to make, the two men sat before the fire. Their voices were held silent while their minds whirled with the events of the past hour.

Zac's goal in the purchase of his small ranch had been to enjoy some solitude and quietness. His still healing soul needed those things. But now, much to his distaste and disappointment, he had pulled trigger on a living being again. On two living beings. Both wounded men were trussed up, lying on clean hay in the barn. They would be lifted into their saddles and carried down to Las Vegas in the morning. Or whenever the clouds broke to allow the drying, warming sun to appear again.

Zac hated the violence life sometimes brought his way. Had hated it from his first day in the gray uniform, years before. It was the indescribable violence and grimness of war that had changed him from the quiet, contented young family man into a warrior determined to win at all costs. Along the way the events of life had exacted a heavy toll.

His troubled memories continued to exact a

price; a price that cost him untold days of deep despair and many nights of sleep, hearing again the thunder of the cannon and the screams of the fallen.

Bouts of dreadful melancholy, and terrible nightmares had grown in him over the months and years of fighting. They followed him still.

Then, to arrive home from the final defeat to discover that his wife and daughter, as well as his parents, had all been murdered by rampaging thugs calling themselves patriots, came near to pushing him into an unrecoverable darkness.

Hard work, determination, adventure and good friends had laid before him a path to survival, if not healing. It had also led him into a comfortable financial position, where he could work, or take his ease, at his own discretion.

Perhaps the biggest boost to his survival was a simple question, a challenge really, asked by his pastor friend, standing at the graves of his family, back in Carob, Texas.

"Is it still well with your soul, my friend?" asked Rev. Moody Tomlinson.

Zac had faced the question with silence. At that time, he was afraid to give an honest answer. Or perhaps it was shame.

Still, within himself, whenever he allowed his mind free rein on the matter, he suspected the question might somehow lead him to recovery. Perhaps even to redemption. But those things seemed so far away. Out of reach, really.

Although Zac and Pastor Moody had parted several years before, the question, never totally answered, came back to Zac's mind, time after time.

Now, here on his small plot of semi-desert hillsides and gullies, he hoped to be left alone. Or, at least to have company of his own choosing.

He was not a recluse. Not totally a loner. As a peculiarity of the depressions that he so easily slipped into, he found he didn't mind having others close by, even when he longed for silence. He took some comfort from their presence. As long as they weren't too close, and they respected his privacy. And could figure out when to be quiet.

Still, Zac had earned the reputation around Las Vegas as a man best left to himself. Rumors and foolish talk had been circulating for months about the mysterious man who had bought the old Ricardo place. He did nothing to dispel the rumors and half-truths, hoping the reputation would stand between him and any thrill seekers, troublemakers or thieves.

But in a growing territory, rapidly settling up with hard driving men, men who were prepared to push others out of the way to get what they coveted, peace seemed to be alluding him.

The Las Vegas sheriff sought his help with a manhunt shortly after his arrival in the territory. With the successful conclusion of that adventure, and with the sheriff singing his praises, Zac's reputation was established. The sheriff now called on him any time he needed help.

Zac always complied, although he would rather be roaming the hills on his big cavalry horse or reading a book under the shade of his ramada.

He accepted that men, sometimes under the influence of drink or greed or simple adventure, would do foolish things. But what had brought a woman to his gate, on a miserable, stormy evening, pursued by three thugs, was a mystery to him.

CHAPTER THREE

As was Mrs. Gonzales' habit, she gave two loud knocks on the wooden door, with the toe of her boot, pushed the latch with her elbow and hollered, "Yo voy." (I come).

Her call caused the two men to rise to their feet and hurry into the kitchen. They knew the woman's arms would be laden with pots of food for the evening meal. Sometimes it seemed as if the main purpose of Mrs. Gonzales' life was the growing and preparation of food.

Zac charged the little family no rent for the use of the old crew quarters, plus the free use of his horses, and all the milk they could ever want. He also stood good for the monthly account at the general store in town.

In exchange, Alejandra Gonzales cooked for the three of them, using the kitchen in the big house, and kept the garden watered and free of weeds.

Amado milked the cow, kept the barn clean and cared for the cattle when Zac was away.

It was a satisfactory arrangement all the way around.

Although Zac could put enough food together to keep from starving, he never took any joy from the eating of it. Alejandra filled the gap left by his own inadequate skills.

The woman who had appeared out of the dark evening held a small tarpaulin over her head, fending off the worst of the downpour, on the rush from the bunk house to the big house. The much shorter Alejandra was huddled under her outstretched arms. Both women, as well as the food pots arrived reasonably dry.

Zac accepted one pot, taking it by the bale, and placing it on the already hot stove. Amado lifted two other, smaller pots from his mother's hands.

Alejandra, tinier than most Anglo western women, flitted around the stove and the adjoining cupboard like a busy bird. She would soon have the room smelling of rice, well spiced with Jalapeno, roasted lamb, hot with Habanero pepper and beans, aromatic with Chiles de arbol.

The spicy meal would be a challenge to the average Northern pallet. To Zac it was as if it was Manna from heaven.

With everyone safely inside and their hands freed from the cooking pots, Zac turned to the strange woman. Instead of questioning her he simply looked and waited.

At first, she seemed to cringe under his stare but within a few seconds she rallied.

It was the first time she had seen her rescuer in the light. She studied him as carefully as the few seconds at her disposal allowed. She saw a slim man of medium height, with broad shoulders and big hands. His long black hair hung loosely over his collar. A single day's growth of black beard did nothing to hide the sun-darkened creases in his rugged face. He looked tough and bold and somewhat handsome.

Holding out her hand she said, "Claire Maddison. I'm led to believe that you're Mr. Isaac Trimbell."

"Most folks simply know me as Zac."

"Well, Zac, I clearly owe you my life and, along with that small detail, I owe you an explanation. First, of course, I must say 'thank you'. Without your timely assistance I can only imagine the horrors those men had in their minds.

"Well, that's behind us all for now. Come and sit by the fire. We'll have coffee while the supper is being prepared. You can tell me your story."

Claire Maddison struggled to find a small smile.

"Yes. It's a simple story, really. At least it started out that way. I'm not exactly sure how it got complicated, or exactly when, but I'll be pleased to share it with you. You've certainly earned that much."

Zac poured a heavy crockery mug of coffee for each of them. He carried both cups into the other room. He set his own coffee on the floor beside the ammunition box before moving his Henry out of the way and indicating the big wing-back chair.

"Make yourself comfortable."

Claire Maddison gingerly eased herself onto the cushion with just a slight groan.

Zac noticed her discomfort but chose not to mention it. He made the assumption that she was feeling the pain of the manhandling endured earlier in the evening.

Turning the handle towards Claire, he passed her the coffee.

Zac seated himself on the wooden ammunition box, picked up his coffee off the floor between his feet, folded his arms on his knees, and studied his guest.

He decided that, while she would not be considered beautiful, in the classic sense, she was definitely pretty. Not young girl pretty, but mature woman pretty. A pretty that would last over time. And she had the typical outdoor qualities that made ranch women distinctly attractive.

Zac silently but deliberately ticked them off in

his mind. Wholesome looking, although he knew that might not be a term she would appreciate. Nor could the term be easily explained. Blonde hair swept back and bound with a ribbon. Tanned to a golden brown where her fair skin was exposed. Hands and shoulders showing that she was familiar with work. Slim but sturdy, well-shaped figure. Without knowing exactly why, he calculated that she would be competent at whatever task she undertook.

Involuntarily he compared her to his long dead wife. He closed his eyes and shuddered inside, as the haunting memories came alive, and then passed on.

There was silence for the space of three or four breaths as Claire sipped the steaming brew and studied her rescuer over the lip of the coffee mug, before she spoke. Even then her words were wrapped in a small, uncomfortable chuckle.

"You are really very intimidating Mister Trimbell. I can see that at least some of what I was told about you could easily be true.

"Well, never mind that. You are what you are, and this day, at least, I am very thankful for that."

There was another pause as Claire searched for just the right words. She pursed her lips and the skin tightened around her eyes, as if the thoughts were struggling to be born.

"I am not blinded to the ways of certain of our society, both men and women, Mister Trimbell. I am also not blinded to the need for what folks in the big cities of the east consider only as unthinking violence, but what people in a newly settled land know as self-protection. It was much the same at home.

"But I am dreadfully sorry for having brought all of that to your doorstep. I'm sorry, but also eternally thankful you were there, just the same."

Claire paused to give Zac the opportunity to respond. When that didn't happen, she continued.

"In brief, here's the story. I was ranch raised in South Texas. Three of my brothers wore the Gray. Only Ethan made it home.

"My one sister, Anna, came west before the war. She married well. A fella named Walter Goodall. She calls him Walt. A good man from an established New Mexico ranching family. One of the few non-Mexican, English speaking families in their area, if I have that correctly understood.

"The two of them moved some distance from his family and established a ranch in the foothills west of Agua Fria. That's near Santa Fe.

"I'm sure you're aware of the uncertain nature of the mail service during the war. I don't know that it's much better even now. Probably won't be better until the railways finish extending their lines across the country. But we did receive a few letters over the years. Most of them were months old before they arrived.

"Somehow, the news of the turmoil in Texas after the war reached as far west as New Mexico. My sister immediately sent another letter, inviting me to join her. Her advice was to leave the home ranch and its well-being to the men.

"Since I was single and no longer young, the offer sounded attractive.

"With a small, rigged-out wagon, providing comfort and some protection from the weather for just myself, and with a solid team, I joined a freighter group heading west. I drove the wagon myself, although I hired a young man who was working on our ranch to harness and look after the horses. He would accompany me until we reached my sister's home. Then he would be free to stay in the West or return to East Texas. His name is Trig Mason. Strange name. He refused to explain how he came by it.

"Besides the care of the animals, he was hired to act as a guard for me and what was mine. He rode, switching his saddle between his own animal, my gelding, and two spares we brought along with us.

"Besides the freighters, we had a military escort most of the way. We were safe and we moved fast."

CHAPTER FOUR

Claire had barely begun her story when they were called to the evening meal. As was the ranch custom, the meal was taken mostly in silence, except when Claire gasped, as the first of the spices hit her palate.

The torrid taste did not prevent her from enjoying a second helping.

Claire offered to help with the cleanup, but Alejandra wouldn't hear of it. She shooed Claire and Zac away, assuring them that she and Amado would only be a few minutes putting the kitchen back in order.

Settled into the big chair again, Claire picked up her story.

"We were alone for some time after the freighter and military escort turned north on some purpose of their own. They would say nothing about their orders and since it didn't involve me, I didn't worry about it. That was just a few miles before we entered New Mexico.

"I did worry a bit about just the two of us travelling into a new, unfamiliar and mostly empty land, but within a few days we started seeing signs of settlement. A few days later we reached Santa Fe. Trig's job was done then, so I paid him off. I believe his plan was to look for opportunity somewhere in the area. He seemed to like what he saw out here.

"I stored the wagon and team with the livery operator and went the last few miles on my horse, getting directions to the ranch from the local sheriff. After what I discovered at the ranch, I tried to find Trig again, without success."

Zac, becoming weary of this dragged out tale said, "Why don't you get down to what happened and tell me why you're here."

It took a moment and a couple of deep breaths, but Claire finally found her voice again.

"Please, Mister Trimbell, forgive me. I do prattle on."

She took another deep breath, settled herself again in the big chair and proceeded with the story.

"As I said, with some help I found the way to my sister's ranch. It's south west of Santa Fe. Mostly west. Bordering the hill country. A large area known as Agua Fria. I can't be more accurate than that because the trail winds its way through the hills, adding miles to the actual distance.

"When I got there, the place was empty. There was no sign of life except a few chickens running loose and a couple of cows off in the distance.

"I called out before opening the ranch house door but there was no answer. When I went in, I could immediately see that the house had been ransacked. There was stuff thrown everywhere. Dirty dishes sat on the counter. The stove was cold. A pot of some kind of food, I couldn't be sure what it was, had already gathered mold. The beds were torn apart.

"There was no note or any other sign of where my sister and her husband might be.

"I decided to check the rest of the buildings. In the barn I found one horse, trapped in a box stall, clearly starving and suffering from thirst. I turned him loose in the yard. The poor thing could hardly stand.

"A more thorough look at the barn led me to a man's body crumpled on the dirt floor at the rear of the building. The man was middle aged, I would say, and dressed like a cowboy. His shirt was caked with dried blood and his hands were clenched tight, with a scrap of checked cloth clutched firmly. It looked like a piece torn from a shirt, as if he had taken a death grip on his assailant before he died.

"I had no clear idea what to do so I rode back to Santa Fe and found the sheriff. He rode out to the ranch with me and we took a further look around. We found nothing new.

"When we decided we had seen all there was to see, Sheriff García, Martin Garcia, folded his arms on the top of his saddle and studied me as I sat my horse, waiting."

"Miss Maddison. I don't hardly know what to tell you. For sure there's been murder and theft done here but by who or how many, I can't begin to tell. The dust and grass of this yard have a thousand horse and cattle tracks on it. The pasture around the yard is the same. Those tracks lead off in every direction.

"I've seen the dead man before. A time or two. In town. Worked here, on the ranch, so far as I know. Never heard a name.

"I'll have old Tubs come out from town with his wagon. Pick up the body and get 'er in the ground before it becomes any riper."

Claire seemed to be holding her emotions in check but clearly, she was struggling, wondering where to take the story from that point. Gnawing her bottom lip, she was pleading for help and under-standing with her eyes.

Zac came to her rescue.

"Miss Maddison, I've asked you already, why did you come to me? How did you hear of me and what do you wish me to do?"

All the brave reserve Clair had been able to call up from some well of courage came crashing down. The lip biting became a tremble and the deep breaths became sobs. The tears seemed to have a will of their own.

Zac had no defence at all against such as that. Much more gently he said again, "Just tell me what you want to do Miss Maddison. In the clearest possible terms."

"Well, first Zac," she sobbed, "It would be easier if you would call me Claire. Miss Maddison makes me sound like a total stranger. Which I guess I really am. But after the matter out on the trail and with those men lying wounded in the barn, I think there is something between us. A bit of familiarity would make my request so much easier to make."

Zac didn't chuckle or show any sign of amusement, except a small smile.

"Alright, Claire. Again, please tell me what you wish from me."

Claire sniffled and tried to wipe her eyes with the sleeve of the shirt she had borrowed from the much smaller Alejandra. The short sleeves came just halfway below Claire's elbows, but she managed to use them to wipe the worst of the dripping tears.

Feeling that this man sitting before her represented her best hope of finding her sister she blurted out, "I need to find my sister and her husband. I couldn't live with myself if I didn't at least try. The sheriff gave me no hope or encouragement but when I kept pestering him, he finally gave me your name. Told me where you lived. Said if you wouldn't help me that I should go back to Texas and forget about it all. I really need your help. Please,

Zak. Will you help me?"

It was all said like one long sentence, with hardly a breath taken.

When Claire was again silent, the two strangers sat looking at each other, the talking done and finished.

"I think so Mister Zac, he will help you. You have come to the right place. Mister Zac is a good man. He help."

Neither Zac nor Claire had taken note of the approach of Alejandra.

Zac looked from one woman to the other, wondering if they had planned all this out before they came to the ranch house for the evening meal. Deciding that it was unlikely, and not knowing what else to do, he stood and reached for his hat and then the Henry.

"I'm going to check on the stock. And the prisoners. We'll talk in the morning. Four bedrooms in this house. First down the hall is mine. You claim any of the others as suits you. Alejandra will help you get settled in. Books on the shelf behind you if you want to sit a while longer. Still coffee in the pot."

With that Zac stepped to the door, pulled his slicker off the wall peg, changed his shoes for boots and went into the night.

CHAPTER FIVE

The eastern sky was showing just the barest slice of the new morning's red dawn when Zac entered the house, kicked his boots off at the door and hung up his hat. The rain had stopped sometime during the night, the skies were clear, but the yard was still a wallow of mud.

Zac had been up before the first light of dawn greeted the new day, seeing to the few necessary ranch chores and preparing to ride.

He addressed the two women who were seated at the table, their breakfasts half-eaten before them.

"We're saddled and ready to ride whenever you are. I'll just be a minute getting a clean shirt."

The women looked up from their meals, their forks held in mid-air, a look of amusement on Alejandra's face and a more serious look of wonder holding Claire's attention. Neither spoke for a few seconds. Finally, Alejandra put down her fork and giggled a bit as she looked across the table.

"Mister Zac, when he is ready, he go. No wait. Best you eat quick and get pack together. I make breakfast for Mister Zac. Give you a few minutes while he eat."

Claire was choking down both her breakfast

and a comment. Slowly she forked up another bite of egg along with some bacon. She had to choose her words carefully. While she was thinking what to say, Zac responded to Alejandra.

"I'm not hungry. Just some coffee. We have miles to make."

Alejandra had been through all this before. Several times.

"No, Mister Zac, you sit. I make good breakfast. First you wash your hands."

Claire glanced between the two of them and started to chuckle.

"I think you're beat on this one Zac. You might just as well take a seat. It's still too dark to see the trail anyway."

Alejandra stepped to the door and glanced outside. She turned to Zac.

"Where is Amado. He go with you? He not eat yet."

"He's staying. He wanted to come but he needs to be here to take care of things."

Claire forked up the last of her breakfast. She had tried to think of a careful response and a question. It wouldn't do to upset this man whom she had come to recruit in her search for her sister. Very carefully she said, "I take it, Zac, that you have decided to accompany me. Or is it that you are simply taking those men to Las Vegas before returning home?"

Zac placed the coffee mug Alejandra had laid before him back onto the table. With barely a glance at Claire he said, "No telling how long ago your sister and her husband fell into trouble, or what happened to them after that. They could be dead and buried up some side wash, or they may be injured and holed up somewhere, needing help.

"The cattle are most likely gone out of the country by now, although it's a far distance to wherever they may be headed.

"We'll dump those men off with the sheriff in town. He can see to their doctoring and whatever else he might decide on. I don't expect there will be much ado about the whole thing. I know you'd probably like to see them in prison, but they didn't really hurt you. Made lots of noise and threats. Very unpleasant threats. And I'm sure they deserve hanging or at least a good whipping, but you'll have to leave it with the law.

"Your concern now has to be your sister. If we linger around Las Vegas waiting for the law to act, we'll just as likely never find her.

"Now get your things. We need to be riding."

Claire put any further questions aside as she scrambled to throw things into her satchel and get her boots on. Ten minutes later she waved goodbye to Alejandra and Amado as she took one final look around the Wayward Ranch yard. Her mind was reeling with the thoughts of all that had happened there in so few hours. Still, her purpose, before those men had trailed her out of town, was to seek help. In spite of all else she had accomplished that.

That two men had been shot was no real fault of her own. That might not be big city thinking but it was Texas ranch thinking and she was comfortable with it.

CHAPTER SIX

The Las Vegas sidewalks began lining with curious people as Zac headed his little parade towards the sheriff's office. He stopped in front of the general store and turned to Claire.

"Do you know how to provision for a two week stay?"

Without waiting for an answer, he continued.

"I expect you do. You pick out whatever you think we'll need and can carry behind our saddles. We'll have no pack animal. Put it on my account. Get me a box of .44s for the Henry. Get some extra shells for whatever weapons you have and anything else you see that might come in handy. You've got fifteen minutes. Get a box of matches."

With no further word Zac turned back to the prisoners, motioning towards the sheriff's office. His three bound prisoners kicked their mounts into a slow walk.

"Morn'n Zac. You brung me a gift, I see. What ya got?"

The sheriff didn't bother stepping down from the boardwalk.

"Morn'n Link. Fellas thought they might have a

bit of fun at the expense of a good lady. Followed her almost to my gate. The whole thing was a mistake that I'm sure they're sorry for now. I'll leave them to you. You might try to get some information out of them. I didn't bother myself. Don't really care. Might should have shot them all and been done with the matter. I don't much care what you do with them. Might need some doctoring."

"Where is this lady you talk about?"

"She's over at Reid's store. Provisioning up for a ride. Her sister and her husband were ranching down near Agua Fria. Rustlers took their herd, shot one cowboy, broke the place all up. The sister and her husband have gone missing. The lady came to me for help. I'll go see what there is to see."

Sheriff Garcia rested his weight on one foot and then another while he studied Zac. He swung his attention to the tightly roped prisoners. The fear in their eyes was a living thing.

Finally, he turned back to Zac. Nodding towards the men he asked, "What are you hoping I can do with them? Anything I can charge them with? Being stupid ain't agin any law, far as I know."

Zac pushed his hat back on his forehead and grinned a bit.

"Well, that one on the grey manhandled the lady pretty hard. Wrestled her off her horse in the rain and the mud. Don't even want to imagine what he and his friends had in their minds, but I guess having evil thoughts ain't agin the law either.

"The lady has bigger things to think about, what with her sister gone to ground and missing. I'd say a couple of weeks in your steel barred hotel to cool off and contemplate their sins, would help them towards a better, more rewarding life.

"Perhaps help them figure out a healthier climate for whatever time they have in their futures too.

It seems to me that New Mexico isn't an up and coming place for them to settle down in. But that decision is yours, Link.

"I'll be riding now. Hope to be back soon."

Turning to the prisoners Zac said, "Fellas, whatever the sheriff does is alright by me. But you think hard before you do anything else as dumb as you did yesterday. And if I ever see any of you anywhere near here again, I'll shoot you out of hand."

With that he turned back to the general store.

The sheriff stepped off the sidewalk and started to untie the men.

"You heard him fellas. I've never once known Zac Trimbell to make a threat. You'd be wise to take his words as a promise. Now let's get you inside."

CHAPTER SEVEN

Two days of hard riding with one cold, waterless camp, put the two riders in Santa Fe. They rode directly to the sheriff's office. They stepped down, tied their animals and swung the office door open. The law man looked up from his desk and studied his two visitors.

"Evening, Zac. I see the lady found you. And you've tak'n on to help her. Figured you would."

Zac had been lying around the ranch for weeks. Two days of hard riding had left him a little sore in the joints and short of patience. It was a struggle to keep the weariness out of his voice.

"Sheriff. What can you tell me? Did you find anything more at the ranch that might help us?"

"Took a couple of fellers out for a look around. Found another body. This one was up a small gully a half mile from the house. Don't figure it'll help either you or me much. Never saw the man before. Might have been one of the rustlers. Might have been a new hand the WO took on. Name of Dude Havner, all time think'n that the letters in his saddle bags were really his."

"Any other papers? Any hint on this Havner person to indicate where the gang might have sold cattle before? Assuming he's one of the rustlers, I mean."

The sheriff smiled and shook his head.

"Now, Zac, you could figure it ain't going to be that easy. There's nothing. Just nothing at all so far as I can see. Where the cattle went or where the lady's family might be hunkered down, assuming they're still somehow alive, is anybody's guess."

Zac asked his final question, although he probably already knew the answer. He simply said, "Tracks?"

"Thousands of them. In all directions and all criss-crossed over each other. Purely as a guess, I'm prepared to believe the rustlers broke the herd into small bunches and drove them across each other's tracks as they headed out. They would have brought them back together, but not for a few miles.

"A really good tracker might sort it out. You know, figure the hoof marks of the driven stock from the wandering and grazing animals. But it would take time, trailing them through those hills and canyons out there. Then, when you figured out where they were headed, they would already be there, with the cattle sold off and the money split."

Claire studied the sheriff with a discouraged look.

Zac aimed a rueful smile at the lawman, as he tugged his hat down tight and prepared to leave the office.

"You were always one to see the bright side of life, Martin."

"Glad to help folks. Anything else you need, why you just speak right up?"

The two men were grinning at one another as two spurned suiters might have, each knowing the situation was near to hopeless.

Standing on the dusty road, with their animals' reins in their hands, Claire looked the picture of dejection.

"Is that it then? Is that all there is? Do I just forget it and go back to Texas to tell my parents that their eldest daughter has disappeared?"

Zac dug down inside and found a genuine smile.

"No, I don't think it's time yet for that. What it's time for is to put these animals in the livery and find ourselves a hotel and a good eating house."

Claire found a bit of a smile herself.

"Judging from dinner a few evenings ago, your definition of a good eating house is one where the cook adds just a bit of rice or beans to the chili. We were known to use some chili back on the home ranch too. But, my oh my!"

Zac chuckled a bit and started walking towards the closest livery. Claire dutifully followed.

With the horses given care and two hotel beds booked and paid for, the weary travellers went in search of a café. They found seats in a busy Mexican run cantina and settled in. The selection laid before them was to Zac's taste, while Claire cautiously picked at her food, never taking her hand off the tumbler of water the waiter had set before her.

After dinner Claire made her apologies and said good night, pointing out the lack of sleep on their long ride, and went to her room.

Zac, as was often his habit when he was traveling, took a seat in the small hotel foyer. He was hoping to find an abandoned newspaper but there was not a one in sight. He contented himself with absently staring out the window,

As darkness began to fall, he shook himself out of his lethargy and stood to his feet. Zac was a man who enjoyed being alone from time to time, but he was cautious, knowing that his aloneness could easily invite thoughts best left unthought. He somehow managed to push them down, mostly, at least, during the activities of a working day.

They gave him continual problems when his mind was at ease.

If he allowed his memory free rein, he couldn't seem to stop the images of a laughing little girl being chased across the farmyard by her beautiful young mother in a happy game. The ending of the game for any normal situation would have the mom catch up the little girl, hug her and twirl her around in a circle while they both laughed. They might even fall to the ground, hugging and giggling until they were ready for some other adventure.

But in Zac's uncontrollable version, the game ended with his two loved ones disappearing into a burning cabin, while a band of raiders laughed and shouted at the gruesome sight.

The end of the vision was always the same. He saw himself hundreds of miles away, unable to come to his family's rescue. Instead of saving his wife and daughter, he was wearing a gray uniform.

The roar of rifles and cannon broke the stillness of the beautiful countryside around him while dying men, with pitiful screams of agony, called out to their buddies for help, or to their mothers or to God. In the end, there was no help, and, it seemed, no end to the agony.

But there was always an end to Zac's many visions and nightmares. That ending was predictable and inevitable; deep, deep sadness, regret, hollowness where his loving heart used to be and depression so foul, he wondered how he would ever escape it.

Over the years he had found the temporary solution to his thoughts to be hard work, good friends and leaning on the little bit of faith in God that still somehow managed to stay alive in his heart.

None of those remedies were available to him on this evening in Santa Fe. Or if they were, he failed to see them. He did the next best thing; he went to the cantina, swallowed down one drink, all he ever allowed himself, and went for a walk.

Santa Fe was a small settlement. It didn't take Zac long to reach the end of the boardwalk and the lighted store and cantina windows. He kept on walking, swinging his Henry at his side, going nowhere.

Going nowhere. That thought entered his mind and for a few moments he couldn't dislodge it.

When he left his friends in Idaho Springs a couple of years before, determined to see some more country and perhaps a new opportunity, those good people had wondered why. Only Phoebe, the former slave who had become his friend, along with her husband Lem, dared to put the question into words. Zac had no answer for her. Their eyes caught and held as he swung into the saddle and picked up the lead to his pack horse.

"I'll see y'all again, by and by."

With a gentle nudge of his spur his gelding had broken into a trot and he was soon out of sight. Now, two years later, he still didn't have a satisfactory answer to Phoebe's question. He was simply wandering. Going nowhere.

After a fitful night's sleep Zac rose early, left his room and made his way to the boardwalk. He would wait for Claire to join him before having breakfast, but he needed a cup of strong coffee to shorten the wait.

He stepped along the front of the small hotel, past the three chairs that sat there summer or winter. He nodded briefly at an early rising young man who held a position in one of the chairs.

The stranger returned the casual nod before saying, "Morn'n, Zac. I was hoping to see you before you left town."

Startled, Zac stopped and turned. He didn't point the Henry directly at the man, but its presence was ominous just the same. Wordlessly Zac looked the man over.

"If we've met before I fail to recollect."

"No, Zac, we haven't met. Fact is, I never heard of you by that name until just a few days ago. Then I remembered an Isaac Trimbell from back in the Carob district of East Texas. Wondered if you might be one and the same. Seems like you are.

"I'm Trig Mason. I rode along with Miss Maddison on her trip out here. Took care of the animals, gathered firewood, kept a gun handy just like you're keeping that Henry handy. You know, just trying to be useful to the lady in a dangerous country."

"And how is it that you call me by name when we haven't met?"

"Saw you riding into town with the lady last evening. Knew she had gone off in search of someone by the name of Zac Trimbell. Figured it had to be you."

"You mentioned Carob, Texas. No one in these parts knows anything about my connection there."

Trig stood and stuck out his hand. Zac hesitated, then gave it a firm, if brief shake.

Trig nodded with his chin.

"There's an old cow camp cook runs a beef and bean joint just across the road. You know, the kind of man that believes you're burning daylight even before the last of the stars begin to fade. He'll be open for business. Sometimes has side meat and eggs, when he can lay hands on them. Let's have coffee and I'll tell you all about myself and what I figure to do."

The little food joint was surprisingly full. Zac figured that was a sign of something. He wasn't sure what. There was no pretty waitress to draw the early risers in, just a painfully thin, unshaven man wearing a white linen apron and a once-white Stetson hat.

The grizzled old camp cook was his own waiter. For sure, no one rousted themselves out of the sack at dawn, hoping to brighten their day with the company of a pretty girl, knowing all the time that they'd be faced with something altogether different. So, it must be the food that filled the place with paying customers.

Trig blew across the top of his coffee mug and cautiously slurped a small sample of the steaming brew, before putting the mug down and folding his elbows across the table before him.

Thumbing his hat back and smiling at Zac he said, "Pa had a little starvation spread somewhat to the east of Carob. Deeper into the piney woods. No reason at all why you might ever have heard the name. We stuck pretty much to ourselves. Only went to town for necessaries, every couple of months.

"Pa, he was friends with the general store merchant down to Carob. Marched and fought together in some old matter way back east. Well before the big one broke out. I never did get the full of all that. Some private, family doings, far as I could learn. Anyhow, your name was mentioned from time to time on those visits. Your name and your Pa's too.

"It was said that if ever someone needed something done, something not easily dealt with, something that needed to be done right, the one to talk to would be a Trimbell."

Zac said nothing, simply waiting for more, studying the young man intently.

"The news about what happened to your family, and some others around, spread all over the country within just a few days of the happening. Most folks probably knew about it months before you heard of it yourself. Awful, terrible thing. Common enough though. There was more than one raider gang riding the country, calling themselves patriots. Scum. Not worth the price of a bullet. Need to be caught up and drowned in the creek."

The table fell silent with Trig wondering if he'd said too much and with Zac suddenly lost in hurt and pain and remembering.

The two men were showing no sign of hurry. A minute passed and then another, as Trig studied the man across from him.

Zac sat with his hands wrapped around the coffee mug but was not drinking from it. His shoulders were slightly slumped, his back bent forward and his head bowed, like a marionette hanging from slack strings.

Becoming aware that Trig and some others were studying him, Zac, with steely determination, pulled his shoulders back and sat up straight, like the cavalry soldier he had once been. Still, afraid his voice would break, he said nothing. Two long sips of coffee gave him the time he needed to get a grip on his damaged emotions.

Trig felt the need to speak, to apologize, if necessary.

"Sorry, Zac. I wasn't thinking. I've never been through what y'all must have suffered. I'll not bring it up again."

Zac lifted his right hand off the coffee mug long enough to wave Trig's concerns away with just a sight flick of his hand.

"My fault. My mind takes me back when I least expect it. The war. The raiders. The loss. The stupidity of it all."

After another long sip of coffee Zac put his cup down and folded his arms across the table, matching Trig's posture.

"How did you happen to meet up with Miss Maddison? It's some distance from Carob to the south Texas ranching country."

Trig grinned at the remembrance.

"Pa never wanted me to sign up with the Confederacy. Said it was a hopeless cause. Held a tight rein on me for awhile as I was growing into what I thought of as manhood. Finally, we had a terror of an argument over it and I saddled up. I had no real way of knowing, but the war was all but over.

Seems there was just some mopping up to do, as some were saying. I always thought of mopping up as something like cleaning the kitchen floor, but military talk, using the self-same words, means death and suffering. Usually to the losing side.

"At the first Confederate camp I rode into, the sight of the men and the camp itself told me things weren't going well. I was still sitting my horse when a sergeant, a bull of a man with enough hair on his face to hide behind, waved me over. His voice was little more than a growl.

"Come to help did you, young feller? The only way to help now is to go home. Go home. Find you a good woman. Raise a strong family. Do your part to re-build the South.

"With that he walked away. I sat my saddle for another minute, taking in the situation around me. Then I turned and rode the hundred miles back home. Pa saw me coming and walked from the barn to take hold of my bridle."

"Too late?"

"That's all he said. I said nothing, just nodded."

Silence, competing with the hub of chatter and the clanking knives and forks from the other tables dominated the small space between Zac and Trig for a few moments.

"We didn't get news in any timely fashion in our part of the deep woods. How Pa had it figured so well is still a mystery to me.

"I stayed for another month or so, but the long ride east had put a notion to travel into my mind. Pa and I parted in peace. He even gave me his blessing, only asking that I write now and then. He would take the letters in to his friend in Carob to have them read to him.

"I rode south and took a job on the Maddison ranch, cowboying and working around. When Miss Maddison was gearing up to come west, I offered to ride along."

The two men studied each other again, as if to size one another up. Finally, Zac leaned back in his chair and turned to rise from the table.

"I'll walk back to the hotel. Miss Maddison should be coming down soon."

Trig smiled.

"No need. She's just coming in the door."

CHAPTER EIGHT

Over breakfasts big enough to challenge the hungriest teamster, Zac, Trig and Claire talked the situation over as thoroughly as they could, with the information they had.

Claire finally turned to Trig with a question.

"Trig, I've asked Zac to help me with this situation. But what do you have in mind? I thought you were looking for a riding job. I was surprised to see you sitting here. And now you're talking as if you intend to join us."

Trig was an easy smiling man. He smiled now.

"Well, I've got the coin you paid me for the trip west, although I'd have done it for no pay and been just as content. I've also got the last six months' ranch wages stowed away in my saddle bag. So, there's no hurry in me adding to my worldly riches.

"The news of your sister and her family is all over town. Didn't see how I could ride away and turn my back on something like that. So, I'm here to help. Fact is, I think I may have found something. I rode out there while you were off to Las Vegas.

"Found a trail. Just a small indication of travel through some mighty rough country. Recent though. The kind of trail I might have searched out, back in the piney woods when we suspected someone had been skulking around.

"I'm thinking I'd like to follow that trail a ways. See what I can see. Came back to tell y'all about it is all. Thought you might like to follow along. I'm of a mind to leave out for there right this very morning."

With nothing more to go on, the trio led their riding animals from the livery and were soon on their way. The supplies purchased in Las Vegas would last another week or more, so nothing was holding them back from an early start.

The ride to the ranch was a short three hours. Riding into the ranch yard there was no sign of human life or activity. A few scattered cattle the rustlers had missed in their rush for escape, were grazing contentedly in the field behind the barn. The horse Claire released from the barn on her earlier visit had joined them. She saw three or four other horses, further out in the pasture. She assumed they were her spares from the trip west. She had turned them loose after arriving at Anna and Walter's WO ranch.

There was no other sign of life.

And then there was. First with suspicious growls and then with frantic, happy barking, a black and white mongrel dog charged from behind the barn, his wagging tail threatening to pull him apart, first from one side and then the other.

Trig was the first to comment.

"What do you suppose that poor animal's been eating all this time? And where was he when I was here a few days ago. Out herding the stock most likely. This breed are natural herders."

Neither Zac nor Claire had any comment.

Trig stepped to the ground and called the happy animal.

"Come here fella. That's a good boy. C'mon."

He knelt and held out his hand as a show of friendliness. The excited, but suspicious dog came close enough to sniff the extended fingers, all the time poised for a quick retreat if it became necessary. With another sniff the dog made the decision that all was well. He leaped at Trig, knocking the young man backwards onto the ground, licking Trig's face and wagging his tail even more furiously.

Trig laughed and pushed himself into a sitting position.

"A bit lonesome are you fella? Could be a mite hungry too, I'm thinking. Well, you let me up and we'll see what we can do about all that."

Trig got to his feet as Zac and Claire were stepping to the ground. The dog ran from one visitor to the other, welcoming them to his home. Finally, he ran to the barn, stopping twice to look behind him, as if to ask if the humans were following.

Trig laughed again and walked to the barn. He was out in just a few moments, smiling and pointing back at the barn with a thumb folded over his shoulder.

"Looks like the milk cow found her way back home. Brought a newborn with her. I'll find a pot of some sort and milk some food for this dog. Won't be but a minute."

The starving dog slurped up one pot of milk and then another. Trig finally said, "That'll do for now old fella. We'll put some vittles together right soon though."

Zac entered the house after asking Claire to wait outside. He was back within a minute.

"It's a mess, but I see no threat. Might be we could straighten the kitchen up enough to get a fire going and put together some lunch. I'll check the smoke house. Could be something there we can cook up."

Trig looked the barn over carefully and then went to the chicken house. He went back to the barn and found two metal pails. He was soon entering the house with enough eggs to last a month. He set them on the counter beside Claire.

"No telling how fresh any of these eggs are but I'm prepared to risk it if you are."

Zac came back into the house with a cured and smoked hog loin.

"Don't usually smoke or cure the chops but that's no matter. I'll cut some of these anyway. We need to get back underway so the quicker we get ourselves fed, the better."

With two thick chops each and a pan of fried spuds, taken from a bin of sprouting potatoes in the root cellar, lunch was soon done. The dog feasted on three chops and another pot of milk with four eggs stirred into it. Claire made coffee from the ranch fixings.

They abandoned the dirty dishes in the interests of time. As Claire was pulling the door closed, she took one more long look inside at the broken mess the rustlers had made of her sister's home. Sadly, knowing how fastidious her sister was, she turned her eyes away and pulled the door closed behind her.

The dog followed the trio of riders from the yard. Claire was of a mind to chase him back, but Trig figured the animal would follow, no matter what they did.

"He might help us sniff out a trail."

Another two-hour ride northwest, guided by Trig, through mixed grass and semi-desert country, studying each knoll and swale they passed, led them across a grassy flat and then into the rougher country beyond.

"Found that trail I mentioned just up yonder," said Trig. "I'll ride a bit ahead. Try to catch a glimpse of their passing. All the time assuming your sister came this way."

They hadn't been on the dim trail more than a mile when the dog perked up his ears and dropped his nose to the ground. Yipping and barking, the animal bounded ahead.

Trig turned in the saddle and grinned at Zac and Claire.

"Well now, what do you make of that?"

Claire looked hopeful. Zac looked the image of concerned determination. After a moment's reflection Trig found himself silently feeling the same concern that showed on Zac's face. There was no knowing what might be at the end of this trail or what the dog might uncover. There could be great relief or great distress. There was just no knowing.

In a couple of places, the horses had to trot to keep up with the dog. Three times they sat silently, waiting for the eager animal to sniff out the continuation of the trail. Each time, with a small bark, he bounded forward.

Trig only occasionally saw marks of a trail. He might have sorted it out without the dog, but it would have taken time, with no guarantee of success.

Again, the dog stopped and turned in circles several times, moving from bush to bush. Finally, he charged under a thorn shrub and disappeared down an almost impassable side gully.

While the riders were sorting out a passage, they heard frantic, excited barking a hundred yards up the gully.

Zac stepped off his horse and tied it to a stout limb. Turning back to the gully he finally found where some brush had been eased aside and then carefully pushed back into place. There was some fresh white wood showing on several branches where the stiff limbs had broken.

Zac forced his way through the brush with no concern for concealment. Stepping into the small gully he spoke over his shoulder.

"You two stay here until I look this over."

As usual, Zac's Henry led the way as he cautiously studied the hoof marked trail.

CHAPTER NINE

With a shout of 'all clear' from Zac, Trig moved forward, leading Zac's mount behind him. Soon they were greeted by a weak, raspy shout of joy. Claire shot past Trig, pulling her horse to a sliding stop before the mouth of a rocky overhang, then leaped from the saddle.

"Anna. Anna. Is that really you?"

Anna fell into her sister's arms and wept. The two women hugged wordlessly until Claire asked, "Where's Walter?"

Anna turned and wordlessly climbed back up the short stone rise that led to the level area above. Claire and Trig followed. Anna sank to the ground on her knees, weeping grievously. Trig figured the weeping was a combination of joy at being rescued and deep caring for the sick and wounded man on the ground before them.

Zac was scouting the area, looking for any sign of trouble.

Lying on a torn-in-half saddle blanket with the other half pulled over his shoulders and around his chest, the wounded man looked grimly at the visitors. A carbine lay within easy reach but clearly, he would be powerless to rise or defend either himself or his wife. He seemed unable to talk.

Anna turned her eyes to Claire and indicated the man lying on the rough bed. She couldn't speak through the sobs and the parched throat that hadn't seen water in far too long.

Claire knelt beside the man.

"I'm Claire. Anna's sister. These men with me have come to help. I'm assuming you're Walter. It's good to meet my brother-in-law, even in these difficult circumstances."

The man simply nodded. No words escaped his dry throat. His eyes seemed out of focus.

Trig, seeing right away that there was no food or water in the small camp, climbed back down to his horse and brought up a canteen. He held it to the woman's mouth, telling her to take it easy with the first sip. Anna half filled her mouth with the tepid liquid and burst into more tears.

Trig wondered if these people had been all this time with no water. He could plainly see that they had no food or any way of cooking it, if they should somehow manage to gather something edible. The old stories were rife with tales of folks who had gone many days without food. But to be this long without water was to defy death.

Trig then knelt beside the wounded man. He lifted his head enough to allow him to drink.

"Take it easy there, fella. Just a sip. Slosh it around your mouth before you swallow. There's enough and more. You can have all you need but we'll go slow at first. Get you some grub right away too.

"I heard you called Walter. I'm known as Trig. Came west as escort to Miss Maddison. The other fella is Zac Trimbell. Hired on for no pay to help track y'all down. Glad we found you. We'll get you back to the ranch by 'n by."

He stood and offered the canteen back to Anna. Following Trig's advice to her husband she thoroughly wet the inside of her mouth, holding the precious liquid for several seconds before swallowing.

"Thank you. We've been desperate for food and water."

Her voice was still scratchy and hoarse. She had taken a seat beside her husband, holding the canteen for him. Claire wasn't sure she would be able to rise again, in her weakened condition, even if she wanted to.

Claire looked around the small space.

"Exactly what did you use for food and water? I see nothing close by."

"We've had no food. No water either. At least none to speak of.

"When I saw a gang of rough looking men riding at full gallop down the slope to the ranch yard, I knew we had to escape. I ran to the barn and screamed for Walter. He was forking hay in the loft and hadn't seen the men rushing towards the yard. Walter managed to get a saddle on my mount but by then there were men riding right up to the house. Walter somehow got a bridle on his animal but there was no time for a saddle. He leaped on bareback. We tore out the back door of the barn and rode for our very lives."

Zac had walked back up to the rocky shelf. Being his usual matter of fact self, he asked, "What happened to your husband?"

Anna looked down at the suffering man and answered, "Most of the men had run into the house but two of them noticed us riding towards the bush. They set out after us. It was a tight go for the first half mile but when it became obvious that we were outdistancing the two who were chasing us, one of them dismounted and pulled his rifle. I was frantic with fear and couldn't stop looking back.

"I saw the man lift his rifle to his shoulder and lay it over his saddle. He only shot twice. Anyway, that's all the shots I heard. The first shot must have been a clear miss, but the second took Walter in the back, just above his hip. A bit further in and I'm sure he would have been killed. I don't understand much about our innards, but the bullet didn't seem to hit anything of a killing nature. It went right through, leaving two awful wounds.

"The problem was the blood. He bled so badly. I was again terrified. We had nothing to help, nothing to work with. We'd had no time to grab anything but the horses.

"I could see Walter weakening and suggested stopping. But we weren't sure the men chasing us had really gone back, and we were in the middle of a grassy plain. We could be seen for over a mile."

Anna seemed to be lost in a desperate memory. Claire took Trig's empty canteen from her and passed her a full one. The weary woman took another sip, got control of herself and continued the story.

"Walter waved one arm at me. 'Ride', he hollered. 'Ride. Don't stop. Don't wait for me.' I did ride and Walter somehow managed to keep up."

Again, she gulped air, more than breathed it.

"We rode until we were in the hills. The horses were lathered and starting to stagger. Walter was lying with his arms wrapped around the horse's neck, with a sturdy grasp on the reins. When a stupid jackrabbit bounded out of a prickly pear patch Walter's horse shied and leaped to the left. Walter went off in an awful tumble. I thought he must have killed himself for sure.

"It took me a bit of time to get my animal stopped and turned around. Walter was a crumpled heap on the ground. But somehow, he was still gripping the reins, so the horse was unable to run off."

Claire considered the distance they had covered, riding from the grassy plain to this hidden gulley in the rough hills.

"How did you get way back in here?"

"With me lifting and Walter taking a grip on the stirrup of my horse, he managed to pull himself to his feet. To one foot I should say. The other leg is broken. I think his hip might be broken too. I can't imagine what pain he forced himself to endure.

"With the help of a steady horse, with me lifting again and Walter suffering terrible agony, we got him lying across the saddle. We rode three or four more hours, with Walter hovering between consciousness and unconsciousness, while I gripped him as best I could, riding his skittish animal alongside him.

"Getting into this gully and up that little bank was pure hell, but Walter managed to crawl on one leg and pull the other along, most of the way. I went back to straighten up the bushes and we've been here ever since.

"I turned the horses loose. The saddle and bridles are stashed under some brush out there somewhere." She waved her arm towards the gully entrance.

"A couple of days later I prayed the animals would return but they never did.

"It's rained twice so I managed to get enough water from little pools in the rocks to keep us alive."

CHAPTER TEN

Trig had a fire going and a frying pan greased and ready. The coffee pot was heating on the other side of the small fire, balanced between a couple of flat rocks, filled with the water from two canteens.

When Claire was free to take over the cooking, Trig went to his horse. Without discussing his plans with any of them he said, "I ain't no way hungry. Y'all take care of this situation. My guess is that Walter shouldn't be moved until we make some preparations. Give me a few hours. I'll be back. Pass me those two empty canteens."

He was gone before anyone could say a word.

Zac turned to Claire with an unasked question.

Claire hunched her shoulders with a bit of a wry grin.

"He's good on a trail, and creative in selecting a camp site. I can vouch for that. Let's wait a bit and see what he comes up with."

With the water, coffee and hot food, Anna and Walter started taking on new life. New hope. The lift in their spirits was visible to Claire and Zac. But clearly, they both had a long way to go for full recovery, especially Walter, who needed professional doctoring on both the bullet wound and the broken bones.

It was mid morning the following day before they heard the rattling of steel rimmed wheels on the rocky ground outside the gully.

"Stay here, I'll go see what's up."

Zac cautiously made his way to the opening into the gully, thinking it was very likely Trig, but wanting to make sure.

At the sight of Trig, and the wagon he had managed to get through the hills, Zac pushed his hat back and scratched his hair.

"What in tarnation have you gone and done now?"

Trig flashed his most charming smile.

"Why, I've gone and brought the latest in traveling comfort. Ranch style. It ain't one of them Pullman cars I hear tell about. But it'll do. I believe it will do. Given circumstances, is what I mean to say."

Zac lowered his hat and took a turn around the wagon, wrapping his knuckles a few times on the grey, decayed and crumbling wood. What he saw was an old, almost falling apart work wagon, half filled with fresh hay, drawn by two saddle horses draped with harness far too large for their small frames. The harness was clearly dried out to an unwieldly stiffness. Trig had doubled up some of the leather straps, tying it together with twine to keep it from falling off the horses' rumps.

Again, Zac took a long look at the unconventional setup. He then lifted his eyes to Trig, who was now sitting sideways on a weary saddle pony, one of the animals in harness, grinning at Zac as he took his inspection. Trig's own gelding was tied from the rear of the wagon.

"I couldn't no way control these beasts other than to ride them. I've switched every few miles just to give them a bit of a rest. It's safe to say neither has ever been under harness before.

"Ain't exactly what the doctor ordered, you might say, but we're here and rar'n to get back on the trail.

"How are your two patients mak'n out?"

Zac took the reins from Trig and tied the team of misfit horses off to some shrubbery.

"Might just as well climb down from that horse and come see for yourself. You're probably ready for some chow too."

"That I am, my friend. That I am."

Trig walked to the rear of the wagon and lowered the tailgate on squealing hinges. Grabbing one handle of a water filled eight-gallon milk can he said, "Grab that other side, my thirsty friend. We'll take this water to where it can do some good."

The two men carried the much-needed water to the fire, with Zac pushing the worst of the thorn bushes out of the way with his free arm. The sound of the water sloshing from side to side in the big can as the men walked was picked up by eager ears.

Claire looked at Trig with a weary half-smile.

"I hope that's what it sounds like."

Trig whipped off his hat and feigned a clumsy bow.

"You need thirst no longer, fair lady. The elixir of all rational beings has now become plentiful."

At the fire Trig was offered a welcome cup of coffee with the promise from Claire that she'd have something more substantial ready just as soon as she could. She had been about to start putting the last of their supplies together for a make-do lunch.

Trig stopped her with, "First, come with me. I've brought a bundle of blankets and a half load of hay, on the wagon. Brought some kitchen fixings too. Couple of pots, bigger fry pan. Dishes. Some other stuff. If someone will give me a hand, we'll go tote what you need for a nooning.

"We can spread out a bed in the back of the wagon when we're ready to go. Which, by the way, I would suggest should be just as soon as possible."

Zac joined him as he led the weary woman out to the wagon. There, nestled safely in the hay was a large basket of eggs, two-quart canning jars of fresh milk, and a whole brisket, filched from the smoke house, besides what he had already mentioned.

Between them, they managed to carry the hoard to the fire. Anna laughed out in joy at the sight, although she didn't try to rise.

Leaving the cooking to Claire, Trig called the dog. The hungry animal switched his tail frantically as Trig whipped up four eggs in a metal pot and drowned them with a half quart of milk. The animal nearly choked getting it all down, his tail continuing its back and forth melody the whole time.

Walter, looking on from his sick bed whispered, "You've made a friend for life."

"Always took a shine to a good dog. Or a good horse."

Trig took his first careful look at the patients. Grimly he studied Anna, who was sitting beside her husband. The strained look on their faces left Trig with nothing he wished to say out loud. 'They're alive. Can't say much more than that.'

Anna rose from the flat rock she had been sitting on. Struggling to make her way down the four rocky steps to the fire, she filled a cup with water and climbed back up to where Walter lay. Retaking her seat and passing the water to Walter, she turned to Trig.

"Thank you, Trig, for all you've done. If you're referring to the wagon from our ranch, we've never used it. Hasn't turned a wheel in years so far as I know. It's a wonder the iron rims didn't fall off on your excursion out here. It came with the place. And we don't have a team, so how did you get the thing here?"

Trig returned a crooked, self conscious smile.

"Well, I found some old harness in the barn. Found those animals Claire turned loose too. Them and a couple of others. They were happy to be caught up. Drove them all back to the ranch.

"That old harness was reluctant to be used. Could hardly bend the leather. But I managed to get it on a couple of nags. Took some stomping and head tossing but I got them to pulling. And here we are. Judging by the squealing wheels the wagon could use a good greasing but I didn't have the grease. Nor the time to do the job, either one."

While Claire was putting the noon meal together, Zac and Trig managed to tote Walter down to the wagon, using a couple of blankets as a make-do stretcher. He gasped out in pain several times, biting his lips to keep from crying out. Anna walked beside her husband with a twist of his shirt gripped firmly in her hand, steadying him on the unstable blankets.

He was soon settled in the wagon, with a good layer of hay providing the first soft bed in many days.

Anna brought his lunch down to him.

Feeling compassion for the animals that had pulled the rig from the ranch, Anna suggested changing the horses under harness. Trig just smiled and said, "You take the harness off these brutes, I'll leave it to you to get it back on."

Nothing more was said about changing horses. They watered the animals as best they could, using up the entire can of water, before setting out on the long trail back to the WO.

Zac followed behind the wagon when they were finally under way. Trig was again astride one of the harnessed horses. Being one riding animal short, Claire and Anna chose to alternate between walking and riding, to relieve the weight on the wagon.

The trail back to the ranch was not well

marked but they had no trouble following the outward-bound wheel marks. Still, the hours passed slowly. On the steeper slopes, to help the undersized team, Zac and Trig used their lariats, tied from their saddle horns to the wagon, pulling to ease the burden. Anna, still weak from her time in the wilderness, switched places with Trig, riding first one harnessed animal and then the other.

Easing the awkward assembly along the rocky trails and through the craggy upthrusts, was a slow and tedious task. But mile by weary mile, they got it done. It was well into the darkening evening before they reached the ranch.

Trig stepped to the ground and walked over to the wagon. He spoke to Anna.

"I know Walter needs to get to the doctor just as soon as possible but these horses are done in. We'll stop here for food and rest. I saw a few more animals running with the cattle as we were coming along. You ladies do what you can for Walter and get some grub put together. Zak and I will see if we can bring in some fresh horseflesh."

Just as soon as he finished talking, he realized he might have overstepped himself. He was the youngest of the group and it wasn't really his show. The decisions should be made by Zac or one of the others.

"That's all the time supposing y'all agree."

Zak came to the young man's rescue.

"Let's get it done while there's still a bit of light."

The two men rode from the yard side by side.

Claire, looking on as they rode away, could tell they were talking seriously. Zac leaned a bit towards the younger man and spoke just a few words. In response, Trig thumbed his hat back a bit and threw his head back in laughter. Claire figured all was well between the two men.

Mostly ignoring the shambles the rustlers had made of the kitchen, the women managed to put a good meal together, cooked on Anna's big cast iron stove. With a two-hour rest and another pair of saddle ponies reluctantly under harness, they got back onto the trail to Santa Fe.

Here the two-track was plain and easy to follow, even in the dark of night. They arrived in town at what Zac figured might be around midnight.

CHAPTER ELEVEN

It took considerable rapping on the door to bring the bleary-eyed physician from his bed. After hearing the story and showing his concern for the time already lost since the wounds first happened, he said, "I've got this stretcher-bed on wheels the blacksmith put together for me. Load the man onto it and roll him in. I'll get dressed and washed up."

The temptation to seek a hotel bed was too much for Zac, Trig and Claire to refuse. Again. Trig took the lead.

"We ain't no way needed down at that sawbone's office. I'm for some bacon and eggs and about three days of sleep."

With no discussion at all, the other two rescuers followed him into the only eating house that was showing a light in the window at the late hour.

In spite of her weariness, Anna somehow stayed on her feet while the doctor worked over her husband.

Walter was eventually put back together to the best of the doctor's ability. He had screamed out in agony several times during the treatment, and weary tears stained his cheeks.

The doctor had told him before he started, "If the pain gets too much for you, I could dope you up with ether. Trouble with that is the after-effects. There'll be no pain now, but you'll wake up with the worst headache this side of the moon and throwing up everything you ate for the past month. You try to hang in there. We'll put you out only as a last resort."

Anna stood by and wiped Walter's face with a cool cloth, although she cringed and closed her eyes, turning away several times as the doctor worked. Twice she left the room, knowing when the doctor lifted a scalpel and leaned over the almost healed bullet wound, that she was likely to faint dead away if she stayed.

The medical ministrations took the entire night and much of the following morning. Finally, the doctor laid down his suturing tools, once again wiped the stitched-up wound with a disinfectant and turned to Anna.

"That's all the human help available to him. If you're a praying woman, I'd suggest this would be a good time to seek the help of the One who put your husband together in the first place."

Anna stretched out on another small bed in the clinic after Walter was allowed to rest. She intended to lay awake and pray but as soon as her head hit the pillow she was gone.

Having slept most of the day away, the group, except for Anna, met again when they all arrived in the hotel lobby at about the same time. Together they walked to the doctor's office. Anna was awake and fussing over Walter, with a damp cloth in her hand and a pan of cool water beside the bed. Walter was drifting in and out of consciousness.

They decided that food was in order. Zac took over the leadership, heading for the small eating house he and Claire had eaten in when they first arrived in Santa Fe.

Claire looked at Anna.

"I hope you like spice."

Anna just smiled.

"Some few things have changed since I left Texas."

Within a half hour they had pushed their empty plates aside and were leaning back in their chairs, enjoying a final cup of coffee.

The café door burst open and a loud male voice said, "There you are, at last. I do believe I've been to every eating place in Santa Fe, looking for you."

All eyes turned to the man, but it was Anna who spoke.

"Leonard, what in the world... It's good to see you but I've some bad news."

She was about to continue but Leonard held his hand up.

"I guess I know the most of it. News took a bit of time getting down to the ranch, but I set out just as quick as I heard. Got in just a couple of hours ago. Been looking for you ever since. Finally got smart enough to ask the doctor. Saw Walter. Now I've found you. I take it these are the friends that brought you and Walter in."

Anna jumped to her feet. After giving her brother-in-law a brief hug, she swung her hand over the table.

"Leonard, I want you to meet my sister, Claire, just out here after a long trip from Texas. Leonard is Walter's brother. They ranch down in Lincoln County, some ways southeast of here.

"And Leonard, these two men are the best friends you're ever likely to meet. Trig, there, escorted Claire all the way from the home ranch. And Zac is a new friend the sheriff advised Claire to look up when Walter and I went missing.

"The timing of Claire's arrival and her finding Zac, and then having Trig decide to join in the hunt, were probably all that kept Walter and me from either dying of thirst or starvation. We owe them our deepest gratitude."

Leonard gave Claire just the briefest handshake, holding only the tips of her fingers, as if he was afraid she might break like a china doll, all the while looking deeply into her eyes.

"It's very good to meet you, Claire. I've heard a lot about you and the Texas ranch. Perhaps when this current mess is dealt with you will find time to tell me more."

Anna thought she saw a bit of a knowing light in her sister's eyes, even in that brief moment, although Claire had simply nodded her head slightly.

Leonard then walked around the table and shook hands with Zac and Trig.

"Men, I and the family can't thank you enough. If there's ever anything, just anything at all, you simply have to call out. I, or anyone on the Double O will jump right to it."

Zac moved his chair a bit, snugging it up to Trig's chair and Claire slid a bit the other way. Leonard pulled an unused chair from another table and sat down.

The cook/waiter waddled over with a handwritten menu consisting of no more than six items.

Leonard smiled up at the man and took the menu, before looking around the table.

"I see you folks have finished. I hope you don't mind if I eat in front of you. It's been a long day, doing without."

He looked at Claire. "What do you recommend for a hungry man Claire?"

Claire laughed a bit too merrily. "I'm the poorest one to ask. We used some chili back on the ranch but I'm afraid I find all of this a bit of a test."

Leonard laughed and spoke to the waiter.

"That beef, beans and rice will do me just fine. Thank you."

CHAPTER TWELVE

After another visit with Walter, which the doctor insisted be kept short, the group again went to an eating house, this time just for coffee and a platter of honey-sweet sopaipillas.

Claire started the conversation.

"So, Anna, I'm assuming you will wish to stay here with Walter. The doctor says he'll be at least two-or-three-weeks mending, before he can be taken home. Even then, he stressed the need for a gentle ride if he hoped to get there without undoing what healing was already taking place.

"Would you trust me to go out to the ranch and start setting things back in order? As you saw, the house is a mess. There's a sight of work to be done. I'm hoping, perhaps Trig would come with me. He could gather up what cattle can be found and fix up the outside damage. He could keep an eye out for our safety too."

Before Anna had a chance to speak, Trig shook his head.

"I'm afraid I can't do that, Claire, as much as I'd like to. But if I let that cattle trail get rained on and wind blown any worse than it already is, I'll never find those missing brutes. Pa, although a scratch farmer at best, always advised that a job half done wasn't done at all. I reckon finding Walter and Anna was only the first half of this job. I figure to ride out of here first thing in the morning, hunt'n a trail to the cattle."

There was silence around the table as the others studied the young man. Finally, Leonard spoke.

"Thank you, Trig. That was my thought exactly. I didn't ride all that way up here just to turn around and ride back. No Goodall, young nor old, either one, ever took kindly to having his property stolen. You can figure on a riding partner. A well armed riding partner."

Anna looked around the table.

"You're fine and loyal friends but I'm afraid the animals are gone. There's been too much time gone past. They could be clear out of the country by now."

"Not necessarily," said Zac. "This country ain't much settled up yet. But there might still be enough folks here and there, along the way to have noticed a passing herd. It wouldn't be easy to hide that many animals.

"I can't think of a ready market short of the Utah or Colorado mining country. Those are both a far distance from here. Probably at least two to three weeks of travel, even if they push the herd for speed. Can't hardly drive stock through the hills and make any good time. That means they'll most likely seek open country. As often as possible anyway.

"There's a sight of open country north of the border but mostly it's ringed with rock upthrusts and forested hills. The thing is, not all of that open country leads anywhere a body might want to be with a herd. A lot of it is just closed-in valleys. A man could find himself driving for miles and have to turn around and seek another path.

"I wandered around some on my way down here. Not being in any particular hurry. Saw pleasant enough looking open country here and there. But it's a caution how those hills just keep popping up at the most inconvenient times. You'd have a time driving cow brutes through. It was no real problem a-horseback but didn't look promising at all otherwise. Like I say, a body could find himself locked into a dead end and have to backtrack.

"If they went north, I'm thinking they can be found."

Again, it was silent around the table. The waiter brought another platter of sopaipillas.

Claire asked, "Did someone order these?"

The smiling waiter gathered up his full command of English and answered, "It seems you have much serious talk. Maybe a little sweetness help."

Leonard laughed. "That young man will go far in this world."

After eating another sweet treat each they resumed the discussion.

Anna turned to Leonard.

"Have you ever been to the west Leonard? Is it possible they went that way?"

"It's possible. There's pretty much open country right into Arizona. If you pick the trail carefully, anyway. Thing is though, when you get there, you're still not anywhere you want to be with a stolen herd. And as for selling, there's no real market that the Arizona ranchers can't already supply. There's mines and a few towns but they have their established suppliers.

"Of course, there's open grass they could claim if the rustlers were intending to keep and work the herd. That's pretty tricky though. Even with re-branding, that WO brand of yours it's not easy to disguise. Big risk of being found out."

Trig had been silent since declaring his intentions to pull out in the morning. Zac looked over at him.

"What's your thought, Trig?"

The young man smiled his crooked smile.

"Well, I've heard tell of men who could track a snake over a flat rock, or a bird across the land by its shadow. I ain't nowhere near that good. Or, at least I don't imagine I am. We had snakes enough back to home but not many flat rocks in those piney woods. So, I had no way to tell for sure.

"Pa taught me all he could and then I ended up teaching him. Funny thing that! Pa, he was a bit put by about it all, but he was proud of me too. Told everyone around how good a tracker I was. Told everyone but me. I had to hear his words from a neighbor."

As always, Trig's grin took away any edge of bragging that may have tainted the story.

"But, how-some-ever, I reckon I'll go take a look around in the morn'n."

Claire smiled at the group, waving her hand across the table. "If we eat any more of these sopaipillas we won't need to waste time on breakfast. We'll be able to get a good early start."

Anna looked startled. She fixed her full attention on her younger sister. "What do you mean 'we'? Surely you don't have some idea of riding along."

"Of course, I'll be riding along. I'm not about to stay in town with nothing at all to do, and I'm surely not staying out at the ranch by myself. I came all the way out from South Texas to start a new life and to be a help to you. Right now, the help you need is to get your herd back. I'll be riding in the morning."

Anna simply shook her head and looked down at the table.

Claire looked over at Zac.

"Zac, what I originally asked of you is done. I and the family owe you a great debt of gratitude. I've already offered to pay you and you waved the idea off. I'll offer again, just to confirm that this is still your position."

She waited but when Zac said nothing she resumed.

"Well then, I expect we'll part in the morning. I wish you every happiness and again, please know the depth of our gratitude for your help in finding Walter and Anna. Please say hello to Alejandra Gonzales for me too."

Zac was never one to show much excitement or enthusiasm. He had long practiced holding a strong grip on his emotions, lest he lose himself in self pity, depression and despair. He was more inclined to simply saddle up and get about what had to be done.

"There ain't nothing special calling me back to Las Vegas right at this very minute. Might be kind of interesting to see some new country. And if we should happen to get up into Colorado, perhaps I'll have a ride by and see if my old friends are doing all right. I guess I'll go along."

Anna couldn't hold back happy tears. She sniffled a couple of times and wiped her eyes with the sleeve of her shirt. She pretended to be taking a sip of coffee to cover her emotions. Finally, she put the cup down. The ever-attentive waiter silently laid a table napkin before her and walked away. It was still a minute before she could speak without fear of her voice cracking.

"Pardon me, please. I'm not usually overly emotional. It's been a difficult time. Pushed Walter and me near the edge. I thought we were as good as dead and then our rescuing angels arrived. I still don't know how Walter is going to come out of all this but I'm praying for the best. And now you dear people are offering to risk your time and maybe your lives, to try to get our herd back. I hardly know what to say. Put it all together and it's almost too much to comprehend."

Zac, even after all the years since the end of the war, had still not beaten down his own inner demons.

He had little tolerance for being in the company of others with a similar affliction. Anna's emotional outburst didn't sit easily on his mind.

The fear of following her into his own deep inner swamp forced him to action; the most reliable cure he had found. He pushed his chair back and rose to his feet.

"You can get along without me here. I'd like to talk with the sheriff if he's still around."

Trig pushed his chair back and stood. "I'll follow along if'n you don't mind."

CHAPTER THIRTEEN

Zac and Trig walked together to the sheriff's office. Martin Garcia was just locking up his door for the night. He watched the two men approaching and finally said, "Just heading out for my evening rounds men. What can I do for you?"

Zac took the lead.

"We intend on trailing those stolen WO cattle. Leaving in the morning. But I got to wondering if there were any other reports of rustling in the area."

Martin twisted the toe of his boot on the wooden walk for a moment and studied the two men as he thought.

"There's been nothing right around here. Two reports some time ago, maybe three or four months. South of here. South and west a bit from Albuquerque. I don't know anything more than just hearsay passed along the trails, but apparently two outfits, the JJ Connected and A-Bar, if I remember right. Both lost large bunches. But that's a ways away from the WO.

"Then there was one away further west too. But that's rumor only. Don't have any facts. Can't help you fellas more than that."

Zac thanked the sheriff and moved off down the walkway.

Trig commented, "Something to consider, don't you think?"

Zac just nodded and kept walking.

Trig followed along silently for a while but finally his impatience got the better of him.

"What ya got in mind now, Zac?"

"I have an early night and a good sleep in mind. Always go for a long walk before bed. Seems to allow me to rest easier if I tire myself out some before calling it a day."

"I'm a good walker too. Walked a whole lot of the way from Texas. I'll tag along if it won't bother ye none."

Zac's answer was to just keep walking.

CHAPTER FOURTEEN

Trig led the group to the trail he had sorted out
while Claire was in Las Vegas recruiting Zac's assistance. Once away from the jumble of tracks in
the regular WO grazing grounds, the marks of a
smaller bunch were clear. The animals were being
driven in a mostly northern direction with a bit of
a westward slant, when the hills allowed. But it was
clearly not the entire herd. Trig was still convinced
that the herd had been broken into several clusters,
to be pushed back together when they cleared the
immediate country.

The first day was slow going as they tried to
establish some truth from what their eyes were
telling them. After backtracking a couple of times
to clarify their thinking, they camped only a few
miles north of the WO Ranch.

With an early start the next morning, Claire and
the three men were twenty miles along the trail
when Trig called a halt. He stepped to the ground,
tied his horse to a small shrub and pushed his way
through a bordering of bush, before climbing the
rocky incline before him.

The country was a riddle of smaller rocky ridges.
Trig, becoming impatient, wanted to see what was
on the other side of the one they were following.

Their trail held the hoof marks of, perhaps, three or four hundred animals. It would not be in the nature of cattle to wander that far while staying in a solid bunch. Trig was convinced that the trail was marked by the driving of WO animals. But what he really wanted was to find the point where the split-off bunches had been brought back together.

He was not long in climbing the fifty-foot ridge. Nearing the top, he removed his hat and eased himself onto his knees. He studied the small valley on the other side of the rise, through a gap between two jagged and broken rocks. The chance of him being seen by anyone in the small valley was near to nothing.

His three riding partners sat patiently while the young man studied the trails. Finally, after many minutes had passed, he turned, put his hat on and carefully made his way back down.

He broke through the brush with a big smile on his face.

"Prettiest thing you ever did see. All broken country off to the south and west. Lots of grass between the hills. Narrow trails entering that grassy valley from every which way. If we were to bother looking, I'm betting we'd find hoof marks in every gorge. Whoever's leading the band of thieves knows the country. Knows exactly what he's doing and where he's heading to.

"Now, we'll just follow this here trail until it turns over that way and I'm figuring we'll see the truth of the situation."

An hour later, after riding over a short hill partially covered with cactus and desert shrubbery, and then down the grassy grade on the other side, still following the hoof marks, the riders sat looking at the churned-up ground that told the truth of Trig's theory.

The new growth of grass was already starting to heal the land but there was no disguising what had gone before.

Leonard studied the ground for awhile before saying, "Probably the most of three weeks ago. With so little rain in this country it would take that time for the grass to recover like it has."

Claire said, "That would make the timing about right."

Zac swung to the ground.

"Horses could use a rest. We'll make coffee and break out what remains of those eating-house sandwiches. If you folks would take care of that I'll scout that offshoot over there. I'm thinking those green leaves might mean water."

An hour later, with the horses watered and rested and with the last of the coffee dumped on the fire, they rode out, heading northwest, following a much larger trail.

A long afternoon followed by another full day of riding brought them to a small sheep spread.

After setting up camp behind a small shelter of mountain mahogany, Leonard said, "I'll just walk over to see what those folks have to say. They couldn't have missed seeing a herd as large as this one. Might remember a brand. That would be a help."

Trig, always wanting to know, to understand, walked along with him. His rudimentary Spanish might allow him to follow a bit of the conversation.

They were met in the farmyard by a smiling sheep herder, holding his big sombrero in one hand hanging along side his leg. A worried looking woman stood in the doorway of the little shanty with four children hovering around her.

Leonard started the conversation with a friendly greeting.

"Hola agradable noche." Hello, nice evening.

"Buena noche sí."

In Spanish Leonard asked, "Did you see the cattle?" he indicated the trail with his arm.

"Yes. We saw. Many cows. Some small calves."

"Did you talk to the drovers?"

"Yes. Two men came to see us. Wanted to water at our well. I told him the men and horses could water, but not so many cows. Our poor well has not so much water."

"Did you see the brands on the cattle?"

When the man looked puzzled, as if he didn't know how to describe what he saw, Leonard knelt in the dust of the yard and sketched a large WO. The response from the sheep man was a worried look and a slowly nodding head.

"What else happened while the men were here? Did you talk long with them? Did they tell you where they were taking the cattle?"

With that, the sheep man looked around him as if to see if anyone was listening, as if he might have already said too much.

Leonard tried to reassure the man.

"I will tell no one about our talk. But the cattle were stolen. The owner would like them returned. It would be a big help if you knew where they were going."

When nothing more was coming from the man, Leonard switched the question to a different direction.

"Did they pay you for the water, or for crossing your land?"

This, too, was met with stony silence.

Trig, losing interest in the smattering of talk he understood, had been studying the layout of the little homestead. He was intrigued by a roughly built pole shed tucked under a large poplar tree behind the house. It wasn't big enough for a lambing or shearing shed.

Saying nothing to the other two men, he began walking that way.

The rancher's eyes spread wide in fear.

"No, que no ir allí." No, you no go there.

The worried shout brought silence to the dusty yard. Leonard studied the man with new eyes, knowing he had been lying, or covering something up. He didn't figure this man had much of value to hide. But to a poverty spread like the one they stood on, anything at all might seem like riches.

Trig turned his eyes to Leonard.

"I'm thinking I'll just take a little look."

The woman called her children into the house and closed the door. The sheep man stood in mute resignation as he and Leonard waited for Trig's return.

Within a couple of minutes, he was back with a big smile on his face.

"A neat half dozen red calves hidden away in that shack. Could be you should ask where they came from and how many times this has happened before. I expect this valley trail might have a bit of a history."

The rancher could no longer hide the truth.

"Yes. The brand you seek was on the cows. Many riders came to my yard. What could I do? I am not a coward. But against so many?"

He followed that sad declaration with an even sadder shrug. He decided to finish the short tale.

"They come. They take water. They no bother my family. They give six young animals, too small to walk so far."

Again, he pleaded, "What could I do?"

Leonard asked his last question.

"Have you seen the same men before?"

"Two times. But not so many cows as this time."

Trig decided it was time to test his use of the language.

"¿Oíste nombres?" Did you hear names?

At that question the sheep man became truly terrified. Leonard and Trig glanced at each other.

Trig didn't know enough Spanish to take the lead. He turned to Leonard with a shrug.

Leonard picked up the questioning.

"You can tell us. The men won't be back. We are going to find them. We are going to stop the stealing of cattle."

Very quietly the defeated man said, "Dawkins. One man I hear called Dawkins. Another is Strawn. They were the leaders. I know no other names."

Leonard, hoping to ease into a more friendly talk asked, "Cómo te llamas, amigo? And what is your name, friend?

"Julio Garcia."

Trig stepped in again. "No más o vuelvo." No more with the rustlers."

He studied the man with a grim look on his face, wanting to be sure the sheep man got the message.

"No más o volveré." No more or I come back."

He followed this promise with a finger across his throat. There was no misunderstanding the meaning. He knew the gesture was useless. Truly, the sheep man would have no chance to stand off an entire drive crew. But the threat might help him to at least stay honest about it.

Leonard looked at Trig with new understanding.

CHAPTER FIFTEEN

Two exhausting weeks of following cattle tracks through northern New Mexico and across Colorado left the foursome weary and wishing for an end to the trail. Only Zac had ever seen this part of the country before and that was just briefly, on his way to the south almost two years earlier.

Leonard pulled his horse up to ride beside Zac.

"What do you know about this grassland we're crossing. The trail's still clear. But I don't see anything ahead that might indicate a destination for the cattle."

"Well, I only came this way the one time. And then I was heading south. I cut in here from a little mining town known as Fairplay. That's along north and west a ways yet, if I'm seeing it right.

"Only cattle I saw were far in the distance, off to the north. And only a few head. I had no reason to turn that way. Saw a few buffalo making themselves to home too. Probably missed by the hide hunters. Good grassland. Be ranches all through here one day."

Leonard nodded at that information, then continued with his thoughts.

"Driving the brutes over those miles of rocky ground showed a desire to hide or confuse the trail. But now it's clear again. It ain't hard to follow. Rustlers must have figured they were out of danger after so many miles. I'm guessing we're coming to the end though. Nothing I heard of north of here but mountains, and mining. Might be a show of grass in the mountain valleys."

They settled into camp that evening within sight of what looked like a small ranch or homesteader's shack tucked into the northern craggy hills. It was impossible to tell what it was from a distance. There were no animals visible from where they rode.

When the cabin first came in sight Zac took a hard turn to the right, heading for another of the seemingly never-ending rocky upthrusts. He pulled up behind the rocks and stepped to the ground.

Not wishing to be seen he said, "I'm thinking we need to be careful from here on. It's doubtful anyone in that cabin saw us. Still, I'm for staying out of sight this night and approaching that spread before first light tomorrow."

The others agreed. They set up camp, making a fire just large enough for cooking. As soon as the food was prepared, they put the fire out and settled in for the night.

For the first time, Zac noticed Leonard glancing at Claire, saying nothing. He wondered if the man had something more than food on his mind. The thought came as a mild shock, forcing him to re-examine his own feelings. That Claire was an attractive, competent woman was obvious. That Zac was often lonely for female company was something he kept strictly to himself. Was he too, having thoughts?

Several times on the trail Zac had seen Trig riding close to Claire, talking freely, but he passed it off as familiarity after the long ride across Texas. Now he wondered about that too.

'None of my business,' he argued silently and unconvincingly with himself.

After an early night, they rose before daylight. Not bothering with coffee or food, they saddled up and prepared to ride.

Leonard turned to Claire.

"No one will think the less of you if you sit this part out."

"Not much, I'm sitting it out. I've come to find my sister's cattle. I'll stick with where the trail leads."

Leonard was sure he was hiding his thoughts about Claire; thoughts that had nothing at all to do with riding long trails or cattle drives. He said nothing, but privately he asked himself, 'What are you going to do with a woman like that?'

The torn-up cattle trail led right onto the outfit's graze. Even in the semi-darkness they could see the hoof marks well enough to confirm their suspicions.

As silently as possible they approached the darkened cabin. There was no barn or other out-buildings that might be hiding a watching man, but the scattered forest rising up the hill behind the cabin worried them some.

Zac took charge, without discussing the matter. Speaking just above a whisper, he said, "These could be friendly folks, with a woman and kids. But somehow, I'm having trouble believing that. It doesn't have the look. We'll be extra vigilant. Leonard, you take Claire and move to the left, tucking yourselves alongside the cabin. You be careful of that window.

"Trig, you swing off to the north and take a position where you can see the cabin door. And, all of you, remember to keep an eye on the bush.

"We'd rather have no shooting if such a thing proves to be possible.

"I'll go see what these folks have to say for themselves. And watch behind you. There could be a night guard out."

Again, they moved forward, following Zac's plan.

As they closed in on the cabin, they could see a small corral protruding from the forest. Four horses had their heads draped over the top rail, watching their approach.

When Zac figured the others were in position, he rode up to the cabin. There was no window that he could see except the one on the south side. The only opening in the front wall was the crudely fitted door. He eased up to it from the side, still astride his trusted cavalry horse.

He reached out and rapped on the door with the barrel of the Henry.

"Time to get up, boys," he shouted. "I want to see you fellas stepping out here one at a time. Anyone carrying a weapon will be shot, and don't you doubt that. Do it now. I'm not known for my patience."

The only reaction was a shuffling of feet on the floor, the squeaking of rope slung mattresses, and several surprised exclamations.

The early morning quiet was shattered by a shot from inside that sent a bullet through the door. Just a single shot. After that, all was quiet again.

"That wasn't no way smart boys. You've got no real choice here. Come out peaceful or we'll burn you out. And I say again, don't you doubt my word. There's graves along some trails that would attest to how I feel about rustlers, thieves and murderers."

That wasn't totally true, but Zac figured no one would question the statement.

"You come out now. Come out with your hands empty, you just might live through the day."

The dawn was barely beginning to break up the darkness.

Someone inside was angry enough to snarl, "Where's that lazy Hoby? He's supposed to be on watch. Probably asleep."

Trig rode up to the front of the cabin just as

the man inside was venting his complaint. He was dragging the unconscious man behind his horse, his saddle rope taking a loop around the man's ankles. He listened to the voice from inside with a grin on his face.

"I've got your night man right here fellas. He can't greet you a good morn'n though. Not right at this particular minute, he can't. He's kind of trussed up and what you might call unconscious. Found him taking a nap against a tree over yonder a ways. He'll probably wake up again bye 'n' bye. At least he might. I had to tunk him pretty good just to be sure he wouldn't do nothing we'd all come to regret."

He dismounted and walked down the tie rope. Loosening the rope, he unwound it from the man's feet and re-coiled it, to hang back on the saddle horn. He then reached into a saddle bag and removed some lighter twine he was in the habit of carrying and re-tied his prisoner, although there was really no need. The man wasn't about to go anywhere.

Zac chuckled a bit at Trig's actions although he wasn't normally the chuckling kind. Turning back to the door he said, "Last chance. The only way any of you have a future to look forward to is to come out peacefully."

Finally, someone inside shouted out, "Private property here, men. There's no way through those hills yonder that would attract a traveler, and we ain't receiving visitors. Best you turn back and go around."

Zac tilted the muzzle of the Henry just a bit and put four bullets through the wall and two through the door. He held his shots high, hoping to stay above the men's heads.

As the shots echoed around the small hollow the cabin was nestled into, Zac began re-loading his weapon.

Several terrified shouts came from the inside.

Each one drowning out the others. Finally, a clear voice said, "Alright, hold on. I'm going to open the door. Don't you shoot me."

One by one, three unshaven, longhaired men came through the door, each wearing nothing but their long Johns. They held their hands at shoulder level, peering into the early dawn to see who was calling them out.

Zac said, "Each of you step to the ground and turn around slowly, so's I can see what weapons you might have stashed away. Still too dark to see real good so don't you push my trust. Any wrong move will have your buddies digging a spot for you."

Slowly they did as they were told. Zac seemed satisfied.

"Alright. Now, I want one of you to go back in and light a lamp. I need to see there's no more of you in there. While you're there, pull some pants on. We have a lady with us. I'm going to ask you to respect her in every way."

A large man, acting like he might be the foreman of the outfit, nodded to the younger of the trio.

With no words exchanged, the young man returned to the cabin. Leaving the door open, he lit a lamp and then reached for his clothes. Zac stepped down from the gelding and took up a position on the top step, just to the side of the door, so he could see inside. The cabin was nothing more than a single room. It was obvious there was no one else present.

With the three men dressed and sitting on the ground, Zac went into the cabin and did a thorough search. He found nothing that wouldn't be found in any bunk house across the west. He brought out a length of rope and threw it to Trig. The prisoners were soon tied and sitting in the grass.

With the morning light now providing easy riding conditions, Zac said, "Leonard I'd like it if you and Claire would stay here. Keep yourselves armed and awake. Trig and I will take a little peek through that gap in the bush."

CHAPTER SIXTEEN

A long, roughly trimmed pine pole had been placed across the opening. Trig dismounted and drew it aside. Once through the brushy gap the area opened into a space of several hundred acres, broken here and there by forest and the ever-present rocky upthrusts.

A full hour went past before the two men returned. They went directly to the unhappy prisoners sitting on the ground.

"Well, fellas. You lied to us at least once. We found the trail out to the north. You did a fair to middling job of closing it up and disguising it. I expect that gap opens up a bit further on, connecting with trails to the gold fields. Would one of you like to say something about that?"

When no one spoke Zac said, "Well, we'll see about that bye 'n' bye. Now, you can plainly see that we've got you, fair and square. I'm guessing that none of you rank any higher than rider or drover in this little rustling game.

"Oh, yes, it's clearly a rustling game. All the cattle we saw are branded WO. That's the herd we've been following all the many miles from Santa Fe. But I doubt if it's your show. It could be that we'll work something out if you just tell us the whole story."

Leonard came from the cabin and spoke to the group.

"You men can think on that while you take on some chuck. Don't know exactly why, but the lady made enough for all of us. Me? I'd have left you to starve.

"Y'all just sit quiet like and I'll bring a plate out for you. Trig will untie one hand only. You do anything foolish I just may take a notion to drag you out into that bush and hang you. Helped hang a couple of rustlers a few years back. That was down in Lincoln County. Believe me men, it's no way to go. You want to avoid that if possible. Best way to do that is to sit quietly by and get ready to tell us the whole story."

With everyone fed and the men again prodded to tell their story, the two smaller prisoners looked to the big man that Zac had guessed was the foreman or leader. Clearly, they had decided to tell their story.

"Name's Randy. You're think'n we're rustlers. We ain't. Not really, we ain't. What we were, was hungry and desperate. We had our suspicions about this outfit right from the start. But a hungry man will do almost anything for food."

The captors studied the four men on the ground. Randy was a large man, broad of face and thick through the shoulders. He had the features of a farming homesteader more than a rider.

Pete and Smiley could have been brothers judging only by looks. Tall, at five foot and eleven inches, with broad shoulders and narrow waists. But there the similarities ended. Pete had a mop of black, curly hair topping off a black beard that was in serious need of trimming. Smiley had eaten his breakfast with the largest hand Zac had ever seen. The fork he ate with looked like a child's toy in his long fingers. He too, needed to give his beard attention. Unlike Pete, Smiley's hair was long and blond and straight, hanging well below his shirt top.

Randy continued their story.

"Rode north from a cattle outfit down in the Panhandle. That was the most of a year ago. We was figur'n on find'n gold, or maybe silver, like we'd heard so many others were doin'. We had a taste for riches and none at all for another cold winter chasin' cows. If any of you ever spent time ridin' herd through a Panhandle winter you might understand why we done that.

"We ended up stakin' our hopes on Georgetown. Me, Pete, Smiley and Hobe, layin' over there. Didn't find noth'n but hard work and empty stomachs. And land that was mostly already claimed and staked by others. But we stuck the winter out, anyway, tellin' ourselves that our luck would turn, come spring. And we were right. It did turn. It got worse. Our only choice was to either pound steel in someone else's tunnel or ride back to Texas. We chose to ride. No grub and no money but we rode out anyway.

"We was down around Fairplay. Little minin' town, off to the west and south, just a bit. We'd been talk'n about what to do. Was about desperate enough to rob a general store for food, or go to stealin' eggs from someone's coup, when this fella stopped us along the trail. Offered us this here rid'n job, no questions to be asked or answered. That was the most of a month ago, if'n I don't mis-remember."

Zac fixed an unsympathetic eye on the man.

"Couldn't you see right away that this is no regular cattle outfit?"

"We saw. But mister, you ever been hungry? I mean hungry like you never been hungry before? Couldn't even run a steer off for meat. There's no beef up here, but these we're riding herd on. Saw a buff or two off in the distance but by the time we rode them down they had hid theirselves down some coulee. Wild game all made for the high-up country or somewhere, what with all the miners taking after them. What I'm tryin' to tell you, and what I already told you before, is that we was hungry.

"We took the job on and here we are. The cabin had some fixin's already in store; potatoes, coffee and such, and we shot and hung a young steer. That was high live'n after the gold fields. Mister, I'm think'n you might have done the same as we did, given circumstances."

Zac said nothing but his mind went back to some of the times he, and the rest of the troops did without back in the war. Yes, he knew what hunger felt like.

Claire came from the cabin with a fresh pot of coffee. She re-filled everyone's mug, including the trussed-up men. That seemed to provide the break Zac needed to temper his feelings.

After sipping fresh brew for a moment or two, Zac looked over at Leonard and Trig, and then at Claire, trying to read their thoughts. Not at all sure he had an accurate read on the situation he proceeded anyway. Taking these animals all the way back to their home range would be nearly impossible for three men and one woman. Yes, they had the cattle. But now, what were they to do with them? He made a decision and addressed the men.

"These animals were stolen down in New Mexico from the lady's sister and her husband. Her husband was some shot up in the doing of it. He's with the doctor in Santa Fe. At least he was when we hit the trail. We intend to find the men responsible and do what we have to do. Might have to shorten their life expectancy just a bit. We'll do what has to be done to stop the rustling too. There's been other rustling done down south. I expect it's all organized by the same thieves."

Randy said, "We wouldn't know noth'n about

any of what happened down to the south."

Trig and Leonard were leaving the questioning up to Zac. Claire was over by the cabin fussing with her horse.

"Let's start with names and numbers. How many men were heading north and what names did they answer to?"

Randy knew there was no turning back once he started telling the details of the story. But the offer from the New Mexico group would be difficult to turn down considering that they were already prisoners.

"Just four men headed the brutes out. They was only driving about three hundred head. Just a part of that bigger bunch back in the hollow. Four men can easily handle that many on those narrow trails. We never heard the two rider's names, but the leaders were known as Dawkins and Strawn. Don't know any first names."

Zac seemed to hesitate for just a moment before he said, "These animals weren't brought up here from New Mexico with just the four men, Dawkins, Strawn and the other two you mentioned. There must have been other riders."

Randy answered, "I asked about that. Apparently, they turned the most of the drovers back somewhere south, after they reached this big plain. Said they'd just been hired for the one job. Didn't want them knowing too much, I'm guessing."

"So where were they taking the small bunch after they left out of here."

"They didn't tell us anything. All we know is the little bit we overheard. Apparently, there's a slaughterhouse. Might be more than one. The one, at least, is near Georgetown. Could be another somewhere over east. Can't tell you for sure about that. One of the men mentioned Idaho Springs but I can't take an oath on that.

"Not particular about the source of their beef.

Dawkins laughed about it all looking the same once it was skinned out.

"I'm thinking you might catch up to those boys if you were lucky enough to make contact with the slaughterhouse."

Zac thought it all through and decided they had all the information they were apt to get. He was anxious to hit the trail, so he got back to making his offer.

"I'm leaving out to do just that very thing. Going alone. The other three will stay here. We don't want to have these animals wandering the country so's we would have to round them up again. It's a big job for just the two men and the lady. So, I'm going to make you an offer."

Again, he glanced at his riding partners. Only Claire showed any thoughts on the matter and that was just a small nod of her head. He turned back to Randy.

"You're claiming you only agreed to herd rustled stock out of desperation. Alright, I'll take you at your word until you show me that you're lying. If that should happen, I'll take you to the bush. I'll hang you, and never give you another thought. And don't you doubt that.

"You men saddle up and herd this stock. As of right now you're on wages with the WO. I'm going to ride on north and track down the rustlers. These other two men will work with you and keep an eye on you. Either of them will know exactly what to do if you break your word.

"If any of you are seen with a weapon, you'll be shot immediately. No excuses. Do you all understand?"

The three men nodded their heads in agreement. Randy again spoke for the group.

"We'll stick with you as long as you need. Take the herd back to New Mexico if'n that's what you need done. You can trust me, and I'll vouch for these others."

Trig bent to untie the men.

"You fellas get saddled up. We've got rid'n to do."

With that settled Zac readied his horse for the trip into the mountains. Claire was just tying down her bedroll and an oiled canvas covered pack on her own animal when Zac noticed.

"What have got in mind Claire? You're rigging out as if you mean to travel some distance."

She smiled at this backward question.

"I figure you'll need my help."

"Really? And how do you figure that. This could become rough. I'd never forgive myself if something were to happen to you."

Claire smiled at Zac's discomfort.

"Well, there are at least three reasons for me coming along. There may well be others. First, a man and woman together can go places, without suspicion, where a man alone might have a problem. Second, these are still my sister's cattle. I'll be wanting to see them returned or well paid for. And then, I expect you'll be heading down to Idaho Springs. I'd love to see the place and meet the friends you told me about. Maybe you could dig me up a small nugget to help me remember this trip."

Zac knew when he was beat. But he tried one more tactic.

"I'm leaving out of here right about now."

He lifted into the saddle and kicked the gelding into a quick trot.

Claire laughed gaily.

"You'll not be leaving me behind that easily Mister Trimbell."

With a sturdy lift from the hand she had wrapped on the horn, and a short jump, she had her foot in the stirrup. Within a quarter mile she was riding side by side with Zac.

He had no more to say on the subject.

CHAPTER SEVENTEEN

It took three days of back breaking work, digging cattle out of the rocky coulees and forested hill-sides, before Leonard figured they had all they were going to get. They pushed the herd through the small gap that had been closed with the pine log and let them loose on the fresh grass beside the shack. The herd grazed the untouched grassland for two days before Leonard and Trig agreed they were ready for the trail.

He looked at the four riders.

"We'll put out at first light in the morning, men. We'll take a fairly easy pace. We don't want to arrive at the ranch with the ribs showing on these animals. We'll let them graze a bit along the way. Anyway, we'll kill our horses if we get in a rush. Truly, a drive like this needs more riding animals, but there's no help for that.

"That will give time for Zac and Claire to get back too.

"You did well the past couple of days. You keep that up, I'll see to it that you get a bonus when the job is done."

He looked over at Hoby.

"How are you holding together, Hoby? You going to be able to stick it?"

Hoby, tall, angular and gaunt, all knees and neck, said, "I'll stick it alright. I want to get back to Texas bad enough to stick almost anything. My head's splitting with pain and I get dizzy from time to time. And there's a soft spot in my skull just above my ear. Don't like that even a little bit. But I'll stick it.

"I'm thinking I'd enjoy taking a crack at tunking Trig's head just the once. Show him what it feels like."

Trig grinned and said nothing.

Leonard said, "Alright, sort and pack whatever you can now. You won't have time but to roll your bedrolls in the morning. We've got a long way to go. We'll throw together some grub for breakfast and take the rest with us."

Randy chuckled a bit, the first time Leonard had seen any sign of mirth among the men.

"Speaking of grub. I'm sure sorry the lady rode off. Ain't a one of us can cook worth talk'n about."

Claire was riding close to Zac as they neared a junction. The narrow, seldom used path they were on abutted a much larger trail. There were five tracks leading away from the one main trail that ran, more or less, east to west. Someone had helpfully marked out a rough sign with arrows pointing towards the various settlements and mines. Zac and Claire stopped and dismounted. It was time to give the animals a rest anyway.

Claire quietly asked, "How about some coffee. Can we take the time?"

"We'll make the time. We've done well this far and it's not all that much farther if I remember correctly. I rode trails similar to these on my way south. The hills are fair riddled with trails, some of them going nowhere but to an abandoned starvation hole.

"The trail to Idaho Springs goes right past Georgetown. It shouldn't be too difficult to find the slaughterhouse in Georgetown. It won't be in the town itself. We'll watch for it along the way.

"I'll stake out the horses."

Claire watched Zac walk away, the reins of a horse in each hand. Although he had been trying to hide it over the past couple of weeks, she had become aware that he was limping. Today he was clearly having trouble putting one foot in front of another. When he returned to the small fire she pointed with an open hand.

"You ever going to tell me what that limp is all about?"

"Probably not."

Claire grinned up at him from her squatting position beside the fire.

"Well, I suppose you don't really have to. A man has the right to hold a secret. Mind, we might be able to adjust our riding a bit if it would relieve the aggravation. Up to you."

Zac chose not to respond. He had no intention of getting more personal with this woman than he already was. He pushed down the brief and unwelcome thoughts that had been teasing his mind a few days ago. But there was no denying that the sight of Leonard and Claire showing a bright friendship as they rode or visited together had awakened feelings that had been carefully dampened down since leaving Carob, Texas.

"Not worth talking about."

With another hour's ride they were within sight of Georgetown. Claire looked over the surrounding countryside and down into the valley where the mining town sat nestled between the peaks.

"I've never seen a mining town before. Is this about average?"

"Well, I've only seen a few myself but they do all appear to be about the same. Lots of activity. Riches for those who struck good pay-dirt. Broken dreams for those who washed out."

Claire looked a bit wistful as she considered that. "Like those Texas cowboys back with the herd."

Zac just nodded his head. He was busy scanning the trail ahead, hoping to see some sign of a slaughterhouse. The hoof-churned trail told them they were still on the right road.

They were within easy riding distance of the town when a smaller, but still much-used trail veered off to the south, through a treelined coulee. Rough with wagon wheel tracks imbedded into soil churned up by the passage of both cattle and horses, it would be difficult to miss. With no words spoken, the two riders turned in.

The trail wound around a brush shrouded hillside and into a small, grass covered valley. At least Zac decided it was probably grass covered before several hundred animals had been enclosed with a sturdy rail fence.

Zac and Claire pulled to a stop at the crest of the short slope leading to what was clearly a slaughterhouse operation.

They had been alerted by the rank odor of blood, death and decay before they rode over the crest of the small ridge. Now, with the bawling of two hundred, mostly red-haired cattle and the shouts of men on horseback separating and driving animals into a large wooden building, there was no doubt about what they were looking at.

They were too far away to see brands clearly, but Zac didn't need the brands before he declared. "Well, there's a few of your sister's cattle."

As Leonard had done back at the rustler's cabin, Zac said, "You could stay here if you wished. That's a rough looking operation, even without the fact they're slaughtering stolen animals. Might not be a great place for a lady."

Claire showed her anger as she watched the mounted men drive another of the WO animals into the killing shed.

The poor brute was balking and bawling, but to no avail. A single shot by an unseen gunman dropped the animal to its knees and then to its side. A chain was draped over the hind legs, just above the hooves. The shackles were pulled tight and then clamped securely by a worker. With the sounds of a small steam engine in the background, a pully turned, tightening the chain. With much clanking as the chain was wound in, the animals hind feet rose from the mud and filth of the yard, then the legs and hind quarters. In just a matter of seconds the carcass was suspended several feet in the air. One of the men lifted a large knife from a scabbard on his belt. With two quick slashes, blood was pouring onto the ground to mix with the quagmire that was already there. The men stood still for only a short minute while the animal bled out. Two men then pushed it along a track and into the larger building.

Zac ground his teeth together at the sight, while Claire's anger grew.

Without a word, Claire drove her horse slowly down the grade towards the slaughter operation. Zac followed, wondering if he was going to be able to keep this headstrong woman out of danger.

CHAPTER EIGHTEEN

In the few minutes it took to ride to the slaughter-house, Zac pondered on the most effective approach to the situation. His first thought was that walking into the operation carrying his Henry might unnecessarily aggravate whoever was there. And he had his Colt in the belt holster in case of need.

But still, this was a business built on stolen beef. The men in charge weren't likely going to be teaching Sunday School on the weekends.

In addition to his own uncertainty, he had no idea what Claire might do.

He had rarely been separated from the Henry since riding home after the war. He found the feel of the hardwood stock and the finely crafted mechanism to be a comfort to him. He was riding with it resting across his thighs now.

While one part of his mind was still grappling with the question, he swung off the horse, stepping to the ground with the Henry in his right hand. Long habit had made the decision for him. He mentally shrugged and tied the animal.

When he turned to help Claire, she was already on the ground. She was carrying her carbine. As Zac took the reins from her hand, he thought he had never seen a woman so angry or so determined.

From the looks of her pursed lips and the fire in her eyes, he figured she just might walk into the plant and start shooting.

"We'll talk a bit first."

Claire flashed him a stern look and stepped towards the door. Zac had to take a few quick steps to get in front of her.

As he pulled the door open, he turned and gave Claire a warning look. Without thinking any further about the best approach, as he had done so many times before, he entered with the Henry pointing the way.

At the sounds of the screen door slamming shut behind him, a bull of a man, draped shoulders to knees in a filthy, bloody, oiled canvas apron, his hands and arms equally bloody, turned to see who was there. He held a wicked-looking, slightly curved butchering knife in his right hand. He did not appear to be happy to have visitors.

With no words spoken, the meat cutter stared at Zac and Claire. He studied the two of them and then looked at the weapons they were carrying. Neither gun was pointed directly at him, but the threat was clearly recognized.

"This here's private. We don't welcome visitors. Too busy. Best you move along."

Zac spoke with the authority of a man long familiar with facing trouble and coming out on top.

"Put the knife down and step outside where it's quieter."

The Henry, and the carbine Claire was holding didn't leave the man much choice. He looked at the other workers, who were all watching, most with the same curved knives in their hands, turned back to Zac and shrugged his shoulders.

Claire stepped outside first, holding the door open for the two men. Her carbine, held on the center of the butcher's bloody apron, never wavered.

Ten feet from the building Zac said, "Far enough.

Now let's talk. First, give us your name."

"Cal McCabe." There was a belligerence to his voice.

Claire held her position five feet from the man. Zac stood a bit further away, aware that if the long-armed butcher thought to make a lunging grab for the Henry, it would be best to be out of reach. He gently put his hand on Claire's shoulder and pulled her back another three feet. He never took his eyes off the man.

Zac simply said, "Well, Cal, tell us about it. Tell us everything and do it quickly. You're butchering stolen beef and you obviously know it. Who's the big boss, the money man? Is it you or someone else? You're going to talk sooner or later so you might just as well save yourself some misery and get on with it."

In a gruff voice that somehow matched the size of the brute, he answered, "This is my plant but I'm just the beef man. We work with the animals the supplier brings to us. It's like a contract system. We kill them and butcher them. We do a good job. We deliver well cut, clean meat to the town. Clean up the killing floor every night. Steam down the cutting room. That's all I'm responsible for."

Zac thought about this for the space of five breaths.

"That's all as might be so. But you still know you're working with stolen stock. Your only way to stay alive, and maybe stay in business, is to tell me who delivers the stock to you and who finances the operation."

Zac could see defeat on the man's face. Clearly, he wanted to stay alive and just as clearly, he wished to keep his business. Zac figured there was no hope of the butcher keeping the business after the law got involved, but that was not his problem to sort out.

The frightened man licked his lips and ran his bloody hands up and down his apron, as if trying to sort out his options. But Zac and Claire, by their very presence guaranteed that he had no real choices.

"Zaborski. Man named Harold Zaborski. Runs a saloon over to Georgetown. The Golden Dollar House.

"Saloon keeper. Gambler. Cattle buyer. Mine owner. Money man. Makes small loans and such."

Zac looked over at Claire. She had relaxed just a bit, but her weapon hadn't dropped any. Zac figured she must be feeling the weight of the carbine by that time.

Zac had another question.

"There were about six to eight hundred head driven north over the past few weeks. Two bunches is my guess. Did you buy them all or were they split among other butchers?"

"There's no other butchers. Not in this area there's not. We supply the beef from here to Idaho Springs, and around the area some. Need an icehouse and such to keep it fresh. We're the only ones."

"So that means you bought eight hundred animals. And doing a rough count in your holding pen, you've already butchered a good many. Either that or you've got them penned up somewhere to hold until you need them. In any case, you bought eight hundred head. At twenty dollars to the head that's sixteen thousand dollars. Did you get the money as a loan from Zaborski or do you carry that kind of cash?"

"I'm not dumb enough to borrow from him. I got my own money."

Claire could see that the man had just trapped himself. She wasn't sure what to do about it, but Zac had been handling the matter alright so far. She would leave it with him for now.

"Those cattle belonged to the lady's sister. They were stolen down in New Mexico, something over two thousand head. We found the others, maybe eleven or twelve hundred head, herded up down south a ways. Now the lady needs to see the money for those you bought. Take it back to her sister."

For the first time, Cal McCabe looked truly worried. He had nothing to say.

Zac let the butcher stew in his own thoughts for a couple of minutes.

A blood covered worker stuck his head around the corner of the partially opened door.

"Everything alright, boss?"

McCabe simply waved his hand, a silent signal to leave the situation alone.

With the stubbornness slowly dissipating from McCabe's face, Zac knew the time was right.

"Go change your clothes, wash yourself up and get your horse. We'll go see Mister Harold Zaborski. We'll go together. Bring your money pouch with you."

McCabe did as he was told. Zac was not an easy man to defy.

CHAPTER 19

Within the hour, Zac, Claire and the truly worried and frightened butcher were slowly riding down the dirt road into Georgetown. The butcher's money pouch, holding just short of three thousand dollars, was safely stowed in Zac's saddle bag. McCabe nearly cried as he handed it over, but he got no sympathy at all from either Zac or Claire. What might be stashed in the meat cutter's bank account had not yet been discussed.

The closer they rode to the Golden Dollar House the more frightened Cal McCabe became.

Zac asked, "Sheriff in this town to be trusted or is he taking sides?"

McCabe answered, "He's square so far as I know. Name's William Broadly. Mostly goes by Billy."

Zac turned his horse towards the small brick building housing the jail and sheriff's office. He swung down at the hitchrail and tied his horse. Looking at the butcher, he said, "Stay put. Don't even think of running. I'd as soon shoot you as not. Might anyway, but we need to see some more money first."

The street was buzzing with folks going about their daily routine; men a-horseback, buggies and wagons of every description, delivery carts and a single ice wagon. A couple of giant ore wagons pulled by four horse hitches passed slowly down the rutted road. Teamsters shouted, iron shod wheels ground on the partially gravelled street. The noise and activity riveted Claire's attention for just a moment.

After her brief look at the activity around her Claire sat her horse, her eyes firmly glued to Mc-Cabe, as Zac entered the sheriff's office. He was back out on the street within ten minutes. The troubled looking sheriff and one deputy came to the street also. The Golden Dollar House was within easy walking distance, but Zac swung aboard his gelding. The sheriff and deputy would walk.

Zac and Claire rode across the street, following the butcher. They tied their animals and stepped onto the walk. Claire took a seat in a ladderback chair in front of the saloon. She did not relax. Her carbine was held across her lap, in plain sight for all to see.

The four men entered the Golden Dollar House with the sheriff leading the way. He made eye contact with no one as far as Zac could tell but still, he had the feeling the man missed nothing. The deputy was more obvious as he twisted his head from side to side, taking in the late afternoon crowd.

From long practice, Zac relied on his peripheral vision to warn of danger as they stepped past the crowded bar and walked directly to the door marked 'office', following the two law men.

Three of the bartenders were too busy with customers to pay any attention. But one aproned man, his two big hands resting, one on each side of the cash register, watched every move they made.

Without knocking, the sheriff turned the latch and pushed the office door open.

The startled look on Harold Zaborski's face, and the man's rapid movement towards the Colt lying on his paper strewn desk, both ceased when he recognised the sheriff.

"What's going on, Sheriff?"

The sheriff walked to the desk and picked up the Colt.

"You got any other weapons on you, Zaborski?"

The silent and startled man simply stared at the questioner.

"Maybe be best if you were to stand up and lift your arms so's I can take a look, see for myself."

So far, the sheriff had not lifted his own weapon from the holster strapped to his left hip, but forward, ready for a cross draw. He exuded a supreme confidence that would be the envy of lesser lawmen.

He glanced at the Colt he held to assure himself that it was loaded, then held it casually, aimed more or less, towards the saloon keeper.

The startled Harold Zaborski finally found his voice.

"What's this all about, Sheriff? You have no call to intrude into my place of business and treat me this way. I'm a respectable businessman. I demand you explain yourself."

Zac almost smiled as he listened to the frightened saloonkeeper try to bluff his way through the situation. Zac was not known as a smiling man.

With one hand on Zaborski's shoulder, the sheriff turned the man around. Quickly and expertly he frisked his clothing and boot tops. He found two derringers and a large hunting knife. He then thoroughly rifled the desk drawers, coming up with another Colt. He removed the shells from the weapons before dropping them into a half-filled trash can that sat beside the desk. With a single swing of his leg he slid the can across the office floor, far out of reach.

Quietly, but with practiced authority the sheriff said, "Zaborski, you're lying to yourself, but don't you lie to me. You're anything but respected in this town. I can't think of a single person that even likes you, and there's no chance at all that anyone respects you. You're a bully and a thief. I suspect you've got a trail of crime behind you as big as this country. I've known it for a long time but couldn't prove anything. You've kept yourself well hidden behind your paid warriors. That appears to be coming to an end."

Zaborski swung his eyes from one man to another. His gaze held on Zac for several seconds before turning a hateful eye on the butcher.

The sheriff talked over his shoulder to the deputy.

"I saw Dawkins and Strawn both, sitting at a table towards the back of the room. Bring them in here. I know they both need shooting. But don't do it until we have their confession. Then, it could be you'll be able to take that pleasure."

The sheriff turned to Zaborski.

"Now, sit down and don't say even one word until I tell you to."

Grudgingly, the saloon man sat behind his desk. He immediately reached his hand under the desk, in front of his legs. Zac was watching carefully. As Zaborski lifted a Colt that had been somehow attached under the desktop Zac spoke.

"You'll die if you lift it."

Zac, having been under enemy fire more than he wished to remember knew the muzzle of the Henry, from eight feet away, would look as big as a mine tunnel to the saloon man. The Colt dropped to the floor.

The sheriff glanced at Zac.

"That was careless of me. I didn't look under there. That's the kind of thing that can considerably shorten a man's life. Thank you."

He told the saloon man to slide his chair into the middle of the floor, out of reach of any desk or shelf. He picked up the dropped weapon and added it to those already in the trash can.

The door opened and two worried looking men entered, followed by the deputy, with a pair of gun belts draped over his shoulder.

"I've had a look boss. They're clean of other weapons."

The deputy hadn't even bothered to pull his own handgun. Zac figured the deputy was as tough and gun wise as they came.

The sheriff used his foot to slide three more chairs into the center of the room. He indicated that Dawkins and Strawn were to sit. The butcher joined them.

"Sit and be quiet."

The stillness of the room was shattered by three fast shots from outside. Zac moved as fast as he had ever moved. The sheriff followed. Only then did the deputy, who had taken a seat on the corner of Zaborski's big desk, pull his Colt, holding it casually, ready. None of the seated men moved or tried to stand.

Zac charged through the saloon, stopping at the doorway to take a cautious look outside. The sheriff, slower to stop, bumped into him, almost pushing him through the swinging doors. Claire was still seated, just as she had been before, but now her carbine was pointed at a man lying on the boardwalk. Another was curled in pain, lying on the filthy road, dangerously close to the horse's hooves. Both were bleeding and grimacing in agony. A small curl of smoke, slowly drifting in the breeze, still hung around Claire's carbine.

A gathering crowd was watching and wondering.

Zac and the sheriff each searched the immediate surroundings before swinging their eyes back to Claire. Zac spoke first.

"What's this all about?"

Claire pushed three new shells into her carbine as she thought out what to answer.

"Well, at first those two were just going to make trouble for me, laughing and saying that any woman sitting outside a saloon was an available woman. I was trying to dissuade them of that notion when Red Shirt, over there, noticed the bulge in your saddlebag, Zac. I warned him off but they both just laughed. I truly hate to be laughed at.

"He managed to get one strap undone while I was keeping this other loser under my eye. Again, I warned them both off and again they just laughed. That one on the boardwalk was reaching for me while the other was undoing the second strap on the saddlebag. I took both actions unkindly."

Neither Zac or the sheriff knew exactly what to do or say. Fortunately, two more deputies were running across the road, their weapons drawn.

Billy, never having dealt with a lady shooter before wasn't exactly sure how to proceed. In any case, the situation in the saloon office was more important right at the moment. He spoke to the two puffing deputies.

"Send someone for the doctor. Get this blood cleaned off the walkway and keep an eye on this woman. And get these other folks moving along. The fun's all over and done."

He spoke to Claire.

"It's a good thing you didn't kill them. Glad you missed your shots."

"I didn't miss."

That response caused the lawman to take a further study of the woman.

He shook his head and looked away.

As the sheriff was turning to re-enter the saloon, one of the deputies reached for Claire's carbine.

"You touch my weapon you'll be need'n the doctor your own self."

Sheriff Broadly let a big breath escape and looked back at Claire.

"Leave her weapon but keep an eye on the whole situation."

Zac had to say something, anything to make folks understand.

"Anything happens to this lady, I'm going to be real unhappy. You don't any of you want that situation facing you."

CHAPTER TWENTY

Back in the saloon office the sheriff had Zac tell the shortened version of recent events. He closed with, "Trailed the stolen herd. Found the bulk of them under guard down near Fairplay. Followed the smaller bunch right to the butcher's doorstep.

"Two dead punchers and one badly shot up ranch owner were left behind in New Mexico. That's in addition to the rustling. Three ranches at least have lost animals.

"Heard the names Dawkins and Strawn from three sources. The first at a starvation sheep spread down south, and the second from the hired cowboys that were holding the larger bunch. Then the butcher confirmed that his supply of butchering stock all came through Zaborski, herded in by Dawkins and Strawn. Has been for the past couple of years.

"Zaborski's the money man. There's no doubt at all that everyone involved knew exactly what they were doing and that the animals were rustled beef."

Zaborski cast a hateful eye at the butcher. He then spoke to the sheriff.

"Billy, none of this is true. And if any part of it is true, it doesn't involve me. I don't know anything about any stolen cattle."

"I clearly told you a few minutes ago not to lie to me, Zaborski. And here you are doing that very thing."

Billy turned to Zac.

"Call those two deputies outside. Have them come in here. You can stay and watch over the lady if that suits you best."

Within a minute, Zac and the deputies were back in the saloon office. Claire trailed along behind them. She still held her carbine.

Billy spoke to the two deputies.

"I want this saloon cleared out and shut down. Do it now. No one, not even the bartenders, are to remove anything at all from the place. We're going to want to take a careful look around when this all settles down."

Zaborski became angrier with every move the sheriff took. Billy looked to be enjoying himself as he spoke to the fuming and distressed man.

"Zaborski, you're done in Georgetown. By the time I get reports from everyone from the Texas Rangers to the Federal Marshals, I expect you'll be done for good. Stand up. Put your hands behind you."

Billy simply glanced at a deputy and nodded his head. The deputy walked forward and clamped crude, blacksmith-made hand cuffs on the saloon man. While that was being done, the sheriff stepped behind the office desk and bent to the big iron safe lodged there. He tried the handle and found it open. Kneeling, he rifled through the random papers and bags of gold coins. Under the gold coins he found neat stacks of bundled paper money. He pulled it all out and laid it on the desk. Zaborski watched each move with mixed terror and distress.

Billy spoke to Zac and Claire.

"All told, balancing the losses and what you've regained, what has it cost the ranch in lost animals?"

Zac repeated what he had told the butcher earlier.

"In a rough count of the animals we found, we figure the ranch lost close enough to sixteen thousand dollars. In addition, there's the time and trouble of riding all the way up here and then driving the found animals back south. There's a value to all that work. I figure another thousand. That's seventeen thousand, accepting round numbers. The butcher donated three thousand to the cause. If there was to be fourteen thousand in that stash on the desk, we'd take it and head back south. Not happy with it all, you know, the riding and the hard work along the way. But we'd figure it for a done deal anyway.

"I'd really rather stay around and see these men hung but we have cattle to drive."

Not bothering with the niceties of courts and lawyers and such, Billy started counting.

Zaborski shouted, "You can't do that. That's my money. You have no proof of any of this. They're all lying."

Billy spoke to his deputies who had just entered the office with the report that the saloon was emptied out and the door locked.

"Cal, Wally, take that man across to the jail. If anyone interferes, shoot him, and Zaborski too."

Zac listened and wondered at the casual law enforcement practices. He thought a court might frown, but then again, perhaps it wouldn't. The country was full up with thieves and wandering grifters. The mines had a way of attracting the worst elements in the country.

There comes a time when the good folks have had enough. Perhaps that time had come in Georgetown.

Before Zaborski left the room, Zac said, "Billy, I have another question. An important question."

Billy simply nodded and waited to hear the enquiry.

Zac said, "Zaborski, I know you didn't arrange

all this from up here in Georgetown. It might go easier for you in court if you'd tell me the name of your contact or partner, or whatever he is, down in the Santa Fe area."

Zaborski actually laughed.

"Ya, I guess you'd like me to lay a name on you but, you see, that's not possible because I'm innocent."

He closed off his little speech with a smirk.

The sheriff said, "Get him out of here."

Billy passed the counted-out bills to Zac, who stuffed them in a large envelope he found on the desk.

With Zaborski out of the room Billy turned to the remaining deputy.

"Take Dawkins and Strawn into the saloon. Don't let them get away."

Only the butcher was left sitting in his chair.

Billy turned his full attention on the man.

"Alright, McCabe, it's just you and me now. Those others won't hear what you say. So, I have just the two questions.

"The first would be, 'is what you've said about the source of the cattle true'?

"The second would be, 'Do you wish to continue with your business'?"

McCabe was anxious to talk. He spoke so quickly his words came out as one long verbal stumble.

"What I've said is true. Every word of it. And yes, I have a good business and wish to continue. But my life won't be worth five cents after Zaborski chases one of his killers after me. I'll have to leave the country. I'd leave today if you'd turn me loose."

Billy thought about this for a minute and then said, "Well, I can see that you might be afraid, but I can't turn you loose. You still knowingly purchased stolen cattle and profited by that arrangement. Plus,

I'll need you in court. What becomes of you after that will be up to the judge."

Speaking to the remaining deputy, Bill said, "Doan, lock him up but put him as far from Zaborski as possible. Set a chair where you can see them all and hold a shotgun on your lap. Anything happens, you do what's needful."

With the butcher gone, Billy walked into the saloon, trailed by Zac and Claire. It took only minutes to get the whole story from Dawkins and Strawn. They were clearly only cowboys, hired on to drive herds. The drive crew they picked up here and there, mostly from saloons, was paid off and released long before they reached their final destination, in the attempt to keep the holding grounds secret.

They had no real idea how the whole system worked.

Billy listened, and then said, "You boys tell that same story in court and I'll recommend to the judge that he go easy on you. Might even turn you loose, to leave the country. Can't tell what the judge will do, but I'll try. You go with this deputy. He's going to lock you up. Got no choice really. Don't you cause any trouble."

When the sheriff indicated that his work was done, Zac asked the same question he had asked Zaborski.

"Wait a minute, men. I need to know who the contact is in New Mexico. Who scouts the range and tells you where to pick up the cattle?"

The two thieves glanced at each other. With a shrug, Dawkins answered, "Makes no never mind to us now, I guess. We've never been there but I'm told it's a ranch west of Santa Fe. Quite a ways west.

"Again, never seen it myself but I'm told the brand on their horses shows a sideways E. It's called the Lazee. Don't know the owner's name. Zaborski's contact is the foreman. Fella called Gibbs. He's not the owner but he runs the show."

Claire had a question.

"How do they get paid for the animals? Did you carry the cash down south with you?"

"We never saw no money. It was all done with bank deposits and telegrams. Apparently, the money was deposited here and somehow drawn out down south. I don't understand how that gets done. I never saw mor'n just my wages, and the wages to pay off the driving crew."

With a nod from Billy, the deputy nudged the two men towards the door. Billy grinned at Zac and Claire.

"That's what's known as a good day's work. You have no idea how long I've wanted to clamp the cuffs on Zaborski. I've got to thank you for bringing it all to a head."

Billy let another short time go past.

"What are your plans now? It's late in the day and that's a lot of money to be carrying. And it's a long ride back south. And by the way, I'll need a receipt for that money."

Without consulting Claire, Zac said. "I don't think we want to give any of Zaborski's friends time to organize. Best if we just disappear. If you need anything from us you can contact me at the Wayward Ranch in Las Vegas and Claire at the WO in Agua Fria, New Mexico.

"We'll be on our way right now and the less said outside this room, the better. It's a long way back to where we left the other cattle, but the trail is clear. We should be there by midnight or so."

Zac held out his hand. The sheriff gave it a firm shake, along with a bit of a smile. No further words were necessary.

Claire stepped up and shook the man's hand. The sheriff held on just a bit too long with a smile on his face.

"Always figured a lady has the right to defend herself. You ride careful now."

Claire nodded and headed for the door.

Zac opened his shirt. He stuffed the loaded envelope inside and closed it up again.

The two riders swung aboard their animals and trotted along the road, headed for the westward trail.

CHAPTER TWENTY-ONE

Zac and Claire were nearing the turn in the road that would take them back the way they had come. After carefully looking behind him, Zac led Claire onto the trail and then, at the first opportunity, ducked down a laneway and was soon lost from sight for anyone following. Claire wondered what he was up to but said nothing. She was twisting her eyes from place to place too, watching for followers.

They were carrying a lot of money. They might also be carrying the futures of Zaborski, McCabe, Dawkins and Strawn. To get well out of town, with miles behind them seemed like a good plan.

Zac, relying on pure guess work, fortified by his definition of logic, calculated that the trail to Idaho Springs had to be somewhere close by. They turned at the next corner, heading slowly back to the main road. Tucked behind the front corner of a closed and darkened mercantile store, they stopped and scanned the choices. In the gathering dimness of evening Claire, remembering about Zac's plan to visit Idaho Springs, pointed south to where a well used trail swung off to the east. There was a sign at the entrance, but it was too dark and too far away to be easily read. She pointed it out to Zac.

Zac nodded and quietly said, "Good eyes. We'll

check it out."

Holding to an easy trot to avoid drawing attention to themselves, they were soon close enough to read the sign. Among several other directional names, mostly to mines, they saw what they wanted to see. Together they rode forward, each taking another careful look behind them.

Zac glanced over at Claire and nodded, as they lifted their animals into a lope that would put distance behind them without wearing the horses into the ground. They alternated between loping and a trot, and occasionally a restful walk. The miles rolled away at a satisfying pace. They saw no one following. Three riders and two wagons passed, going the other way, heading towards Georgetown. After a hard look at each, Zac figured they posed no risk.

Full darkness had overtaken the riders before they covered the short twelve miles to Idaho Springs. But Zac was now back in familiar territory. When he slowed his gelding to a trot and leaned back in the saddle, relaxed at last, Claire took note and followed suit. Soon they were riding down the main street of the familiar gold mining town.

Even in the shadowy light cast by lamp-lit windows Zac could see that much had changed in the two years he had been gone. Old wooden structures had been replaced by new brick and stone buildings. A large new hotel offered its services, along with a collection of other new businesses. Where he had burned down the saloon and gambling house, years before, someone had built a new saloon.

But the old, familiar livery was still there.

Zac turned in, swung to the ground, and bent backwards to relieve his sore muscles. His hip had been thundering in pain for over an hour. To step out of the saddle and get back on his feet was pure pleasure. Claire dismounted beside him.

The same livery man Zac recognized from before strolled from his little office to greet them. He reached for the reins, intending to lead the animals to stalls when he took a second look at Zac.

"Well, thunderation. Thought as how ya was ded 'n' gone. Tak'n away by the birds er the coyotes. Ain't seen neither hide nor hair a ya fer all these many months. I know. I know, ain't none a my business. I'm jest a nosy old man. Wal, anyhow, welcome back. Good ta see ya."

Zac shook the old man's hand and introduced Claire.

"We're just riding partners, doing a piece of work. Don't you be starting any rumors."

"I never in ma whole life started no rumors. How kin ya say sech a unkind thing as thet. Why…"

Zac laughed and took the reins for his own gelding.

"Here, let me help you."

Ten minutes later, with their saddle bags over one shoulder and their carbines swinging in their right hands they headed for the new hotel, hoping for a couple of rooms, supper, and perhaps a bath for Claire.

The new hotel was more than they could have asked for. Their rooms were comfortable. The late dinner was filling and tasty.

With Claire settled in for the night, Zac, as was his long habit, returned to the lobby. He glanced all around, hoping to find a newspaper or see someone he knew. When neither of those wishes were fulfilled, he decided to go for a walk. His hip was still making itself felt and he knew that lying in bed would only aggravate it. Anyway, he was tired, but not really sleepy. A walk was just the thing.

As he strolled the familiar sidewalks, and a few that were not so familiar, his memory started taking him back to the trip west from Carob, Texas, and the events that led to that time, and eventually to this small gold mining town.

Horrible memories of war and murder pressed him down. He felt himself sinking, as he had done so often before. Sinking into his own dark space. It was always a shock to him how quickly he could drop into his own, personal black hole. And he was dismayed at how slowly he recovered. Even when he struggled against the darkness, his recovery was slow and uncertain. He couldn't imagine the result if he simply ceased struggling and let go. Thankfully, most times, his determination was enough to prevent a fall into the very depths.

That brought back the memory of Phoebe. That memory, in turn, made him smile as he thought of all the times that dear lady had helped him over a rough patch of depression, darkness and loss. Hoping to see Lem and Phoebe in the morning brightened his mind just a bit.

He returned to the hotel and headed for bed, knowing that if he didn't shut off the memories, he would be in serious need of Phoebe's help again. His depressions and depth of loss were never far from him. He had to constantly prevent them from rising to the surface. Perhaps sleep would hold them at bay for a few hours.

Zac rose early, figuring to drink dining room coffee while he waited for Claire. But when he arrived, she was already seated with a menu and a coffee cup placed before her.

Claire greeted him with a cheery good morning, which he might have returned had his hip not still been lending its misery, clouding out the bright morning.

"You don't look all that rested. Have trouble sleeping?"

Zac was careful of what he said. His troubles were his own. He had no intention of sharing them with this woman who, after all, he barely knew, and wouldn't know at all except for the stolen cattle.

"I'm a light sleeper at the best of times. I might sleep better after we bank this money."

They ordered their breakfasts and ate in silence, as was their habit. Claire finally put down her fork and said, "So, what's first?"

"Well I'd really like to get this money banked but they don't open for a while yet. I'm thinking we could go down to the law office and talk to Gomer Radcliff. He's my lawyer friend that's helped so much in the past. At the very least he'll be able to tell us where everyone is living. He's also the lawyer for the mine so he'll have the updated information on that."

Claire nodded her understanding but said nothing while the waitress refilled their cups.

"I'm anxious to meet your friends and to see the mine. I've never seen a working mine. But while we wait for a more reasonable time of day to arrive why don't you tell me your story."

Zac paused and folded his arms in front of himself, on the café table. He had started out with no intention at all of sharing personal information with this woman who had arrived at his ranch, out of the storm, gunshots announcing her arrival. He hated talking about himself. He found it embarrassing and a bit demeaning. Especially, he didn't want to talk about his continuing emotional weakness. To even mention it seemed somehow unmanly.

But after a few seconds of silence, while he thought it over, he decided Claire had earned some trust. She had ridden the same miles he and the other men had ridden; taken the same risks. Never complained. Perhaps if he shared just a bit she would be satisfied.

He glanced up from the tabletop to see Claire's eyes firmly on him, as if she was waiting.

"Not much of a story really. I wore the gray. Cavalry. Awful, terrible time. But it seemed sometimes, looking out at the spread-out armies lining up for battle, that half the young men in the nation did the same. So, I'm nowhere near special.

"Started having nightmares and sleepless nights somewhere around halfway through the conflict. Rode out after the last bugle. They lowered the flag and hid it from sight. That was the end for our little part of the army.

"Simply turned my horse away and rode home. That's the same animal I'm still riding. Good horse.

"Got home to Texas, little place near the piney woods called Carob. Found my wife and daughter both dead, house burned. Lots of others suffered the same, including my folks. Terror gang calling themselves patriots rode through killing, burning, robbing.

"Couldn't stay there. Black couple. Lem and Phoebe. Freed well before the war. Good friends before I rode away to battle. They had a team of mules. I had a wagon. Together we ran. Ran from the horror. Ran from the pain. Made our way west. Had no real idea why. Just hoping for something better, somewhere new.

"Arrived in this little town. Idaho Springs. Knew nothing at all about mining or finding gold. Met a man. Polish. Not much English but he made us understand that he was a geologist. Thought he had found something. We took a look and liked what he showed us. Went to work with him. I provided the funding while he looked for gold.

"Dominik. Good man. Smart.

"We found gold. A lot of gold.

"Had a run-in with a local gangster. He kidnapped Phoebe, hoping to blackmail us out of our mine. Dead now. Him and some others.

"Anyway, we sold off most of the mine. Big mining company. My friends are all still here. Can't keep Lem away from his mine and can't stop Dominick from prowling the hills looking for another strike.

All good folks. I'm anxious to see them again."

Claire could hardly take it all in, the story came so fast, even if it was in bits and pieces. Reading between the lines she knew there was a much bigger story buried under this short version. She wondered what the longer story would look like. But even that skeleton bit of the tale provided her a glimpse into some things she had noted on the long ride north: Zac's periodic quietness. His penchant to ride off to the side, alone. The silent working of his lips, as if he was thinking private thoughts. His quickness to violence coupled with his enormous self control.

"So why did you leave?"

As before, Zac hesitated for so long Claire feared he would say nothing at all, and she would be left wondering.

"Sometimes things start to close in on me. It's not like it was, right after the war. I've healed some since then. But it's still not good. I don't sleep well. I still have nightmares. See men dying and screaming in pain. Men I knew.

"Sometimes I sink down inside. Depression, the medical people call it. Some call it by other names. Sometimes I need to be with other people. Most times I prefer to be alone.

"I left Colorado to keep whatever was left of my mind. Didn't need any more money anyway so I sold all but a small share in the mine. Still, they keep putting profits in my bank account. Gomer, our lawyer friend looks after all that. I get a letter from him once in a while. Have no idea what's in the account now.

"Don't like cold and snow either. So, I went south."

The story was clearly finished. Claire leaned back in her chair and studied this man who had saved her life and then found the stolen cattle. For a space of time she was lost for words. She reached across the table and laid her hand on top of Zac's folded hands.

"Thank you for telling me all that. I never once suspected. I've been praying about the lost cattle and my wounded brother-in-law and each of us as we take this long ride. But now I can see that I need to be praying for you. Especially for you. That God might make you completely well again.

"And now I'm feeling guilty for asking you to take on this whole rustling matter. It's been a strain on all of us. I can't imagine what a burden it is to you."

Zac pulled his hands from the table and lifted his coffee cup again. After sipping and then returning the cup to the table he said, "No. You don't need to feel guilty. I came of my own decision. Action is good for me. Sometimes. Helps me break out of my gloom. Kind of replaces my will power, which I seem to some days be in short supply of."

"Anyways, let's go see if Gomer has shaken loose of the bedcovers yet."

CHAPTER TWENTY-TWO

The town was spread out enough, and the walk to the lawyer's office distant enough, that they went for their horses. The old man watched them crossing the road and then stepped into the tack shed for their saddles. By the time they arrived at the barn, Claire's animal was rigged out and ready. The hostler was just tightening the cinch of Zac's mount. They were on their way within seconds.

Drawing up to the hitch rail before the law office, Zac swung down.

"You might just as well come in and meet Gomer. We'll be here a while."

Claire stepped to the ground and joined Zac as he was reaching for the door handle. He swung the door open and the two of them walked in. A harried man's partially muffled voice said, "Take a seat. I'll just be a moment."

His head was supported by one hand beneath his chin, with the fingers laid over his mouth, while he scribbled on notepaper with the other hand.

A scraping of chair legs on the floor and a scream of happy recognition, from a desk in the far corner got everyone's attention.

A beautiful black lady jumped to her feet.

"Zac? Oh, Zac. I can hardly believe it."

She rushed across the small space and threw her arms around Zac's neck, hugging him tightly.

"My, oh my. How we've missed you and how good it is to see you."

By this time the smiling lawyer was joining the greeting. Zac loosened himself from the woman and gave the lawyer a firm handshake. Neither man found it necessary to speak their welcome. The handshake seemed to say all that needed saying.

Gomer turned to Claire while speaking to Zac.

"And who is this. I'm guessing you've come all this way to introduce your wife."

Zac laughed in spite of his embarrassment.

"No, not hardly. Claire is a fine lady and will make some man a good wife someday. But I'm afraid we're simply involved in a business matter. Gomer, Tillie, you need to say hello to Claire Maddison."

The attention of both the lawyer and Tillie turned to Claire. Gomer spoke for the two of them.

"It's great to meet you Claire. I expect there's a story to tell and you're the one we'll rely on to tell it. Getting information from this other big lug can be a bit tedious. Welcome to Idaho Springs. This is my wife, Tillie. That little girl with her thumb in her mouth and her big eyes fixed on our visitors is our precious Sarah."

Zac had no comment on the child, although his eyes were glued on her. Gomer's sharp mind was pulling up the story of Zac's wife and child being murdered and burned inside their flaming cabin. He was sure the memory was troubling his friend, but it couldn't be helped. They wouldn't be able, or willing, to hide their baby from Zac. He would just have to adjust.

Everyone started talking at once and then everyone stopped, waiting for the other. Finally, Tillie stepped into the momentary silence.

"There's a new café just a couple of doors up the

street. I expect they opened mainly for us, knowing how much coffee we drink. We take our lunch there most days. Let's go have a coffee and a visit. I won't rest till I hear it all."

Over the next hour Zac and Claire were brought up to date on the workings of the mine, the marriage of Dominik and Bianka and their little one, the doings of Lem and Phoebe; how Lem couldn't stay away from the mine and Phoebe was busy helping the many poor blacks in the little town.

Dominik had staked a few promising new finds.

When Gomer pleaded that he had to get back to work, they agreed that they would gather up the old crowd and meet at the hotel dining room for dinner.

With that done, Zac and Claire mounted their horses and rode to the bank. Zac counted out all but one thousand dollars, kept in small bills for covering expenses on the road back to Agua Fria. The remainder of the funds was placed into Zac's personal account. The banker returned a draft for the amount, assuring them that the draft could be deposited in any Colorado or New Mexico bank.

Zac then passed over his own account book for updating. He and Claire waited several minutes for the clerk to go to the back office, where the file was kept. When he returned and passed the book back, Zac took a careful look, his eyes getting bigger and bigger as he studied the numbers.

Claire didn't mean to snoop. Not really, she didn't. But a quick glance past Zac's folded elbow was enough. She couldn't see all the numbers, but she could see the bottom one. Her eyes opened in wonder, as did Zac's.

Zac looked at the young clerk.

"Are you sure? You didn't mix up my account with someone else?"

"No mix-up, Mister Trimble. Were you expecting a larger number?"

"No. No. It's not that at all."

Another half minute went past while Zac looked at the book, thinking his silent thoughts. Looking up, he said, "Tell you what. I want you to make out another draft for ten thousand in my name and one for two thousand in the name of Reverend Moody Tomlinson, Carob, Texas."

The clerk jotted the two names in full and disappeared again into the back office.

Zac and Claire made their way back to the lawyer's office. Zac borrowed an envelope and sat down at Tillie's desk to write a short note to his pastor friend, stressing that the funds were for Moody and his wife, not for the workings of the little church. He inserted the bank draft, addressed the envelope and asked where he could mail it.

"Leave it right there," answered Tillie. "I'll send it out with the office mail."

With that done, Tillie provided the simple directions to Lem and Phoebe's home.

CHAPTER TWENTY-THREE

The ride to visit Phoebe took the pair right past Mrs. Templeton's boarding house.

Zac nodded towards the house with his chin.

"We all stayed here before the others found mates and got themselves married. Missus Templeton. Good lady. Widow. I'd favor moving ourselves down here from the hotel if she has a couple of spare rooms."

"Sounds good to me."

Zac turned towards the boarding house and dismounted. He was just about to lay his hand on the gate when the front door burst open, crashing against the floor mounted doorstop.

"Zac Trimbell. As I live and breathe. Get yourself in here so's I can give you a hug. Bring your lady friend with you."

Zac was sure the neighbors could hear the excited shouts.

Claire dismounted and the two of them strode towards the house. Claire gave a curious glance at Zac, wondering how this quiet, often withdrawn man had created such caring and loyalty among his friends.

Mrs. Templeton found her patience sorely tested, although it was mere seconds since she had seen

Zac and Claire from her kitchen window. Tired of waiting, she clumped down the four stairs leading from her veranda and rushed along the walk. The three met halfway to the house. Zac steeled himself to suffer another hug. Tillie's hug had almost undone him. Mrs. Templeton's repeat of that experience forced him to bite his tongue while he endured. The thought of a similar greeting from Phoebe was a sore test.

Zac wasn't the hugging kind. Never had been.

He finally had the opportunity to introduce Claire and assure Mrs. Templeton that their relationship was strictly business.

Mrs. Templeton give Claire a careful study and a handshake.

"That's unfortunate. Well, come to the porch. We'll take a seat. I want to hear it all."

Seated comfortably, Zac briefly explained the happenings that had brought them north.

"I'm anxious to see Phoebe and the rest. We thought we'd visit Phoebe and then ride up to the mine. But first, I need to ask if you have a couple of rooms available for a few days."

"Sure as you know. Claire can have your old space. You'll have to climb the stairs. But now your hip is healed that shouldn't present a problem."

Claire turned her head towards Zac and then back to Mrs. Templeton.

With a bit of a smile she said, "My often-silent friend here has told me just a bit of his story; the war, and all. But, of course, I've seen him limping. Nothing he told me explains that, unless it's a war wound. But if he was healing here just a couple of years ago it can't be that."

She didn't really ask a question, but the question hung in the air, just the same.

Zac stood, effectively bringing the conversation to a close.

"I'll get our packs off the horses. Claire, we need

to get underway right soon."

The two women glanced at each other, knowing there would be another day and another conversation.

Within minutes, a short ride had the two travellers standing on the small porch in front of Lem and Phoebe's house. A single knock brought a very surprised Phoebe to the door. The greeting was a parallel to the two Zac had already received. But perhaps, just a little bit more reserved. Claire stood back in renewed wonder.

They stayed just long enough for a quick cup of coffee and a cinnamon roll, fresh from the oven. Begging the need to get to the mine, they told Phoebe of the plan for a hotel dinner and took their leave.

The ride to the mine was longer and much changed from when Zac had last seen it. The rough, rocky trail the original miners had scrambled over had been rerouted and cleaned up. Three switchback turns reduced the overall grade, making the trip easier on the ore wagon animals.

Arriving at the mine, Zac sat his saddle in wonder. He pushed his hat back on his head and stared. Gone was everything familiar. Where the sleeping tent had been, there was now a fine office building. The original face of the mine was totally enveloped in a large metal-clad building. Parallel rails led from the mine shaft, across the old tailings pile to a wagon loading chute. Several workers were pushing filled ore carts along the rails, as a shouting teamster maneuvered his team and wagon under the chute.

A uniformed security man, a carbine slung over his shoulder and a handgun strapped to his hip, walked quickly from the mine office.

"Can I help you folks? Don't normally welcome

no visitors." The guard made no secret of his nervous interest in the two well armed riders.

Zac looked at the man and then turned his eyes back to the mine. Uphill, a few hundred yards past the main opening, he could see a structure similar to the one right before him. That structure would mark the location of the strike that had Dominik struggling in the snow and hurling Polish curses after his run-away horse.

Zac scanned off to the right. Over there was the last discovery made, just before he pulled out for New Mexico. But it was over a bit of a rise and quite a distance away. He was unable to see if any work had been done on it.

Finally, he turned back to the security man, who had never taken his eyes off the pair.

"Lem around? Or Dominik?"

"You tell me who you are and what you want here, and I might answer your questions."

Zac leaned back in his saddle. As an owner, he took some minor offence to being questioned. Finally, he took a clear look at the guard. A young man, perhaps a bit unsure of himself. He would have no way to know who Zac was or even to have heard his name before. Just doing his job. Wouldn't pay to challenge him. Never knew what might come of challenging an insecure man with authority. And a gun.

"No need for a fuss, friend. You go tell Lem that Zac is here. We'll wait."

The security man never took his eyes off Zac as he walked sidewise towards the office. He made his way up the three steps and opened the door.

"Visitor out here says he knows you Lem."

A big, bulky, powerful, black man stepped onto the porch. A fine-looking man. Claire could immediately see that this man and Pheobe would be a handsome couple.

The reception was much the same as the three

previous greetings. Only the hugs were missing. But, at first, as the black man was climbing down the stairs, his eyes wide open in surprise and welcome, the old slave days habits burst forth from Lem.

"Mister Isaac. Dat you?

"Well land a Goshen. I do believe it is you."

Lem rushed down the stairs in a replay of what Mrs. Templeton had done. Instead of a hug there was a firm handshake, accompanied by long looks into each other's eyes.

Looking on, Claire thought to herself, 'friendships like I've seldom seen.'

Claire swung to the ground, smiling at Lem. Zac made the introduction and the three of them made their way to the office. Inside, Lem pulled two chairs up beside his desk.

Zac started the conversation.

"Never thought of you as an office man, Lem."

"I'm not, and nev'r will be. We have a mine manager and a man as what keeps track of loads goin' down hill. Tillie gathers up the reports on ore loads and product com'n off'n the mill. Keeps the records straight and safe, all down to the lawyer's office.

"Other crew, dey move da gold from da mill to da bank's big iron safe.

"Me. I'm jest try'n to keep da workers straight and in line. Run two shifts now. Work'n all da day 'n' all da night too. I do da hiri'n 'n' da firi'n 'n' sort out when each man goin' ta work. Keep track of hours worked so's Tillie, she kin see ta da pay'n 'n all.

"Don't hardly ever go inta da mine no more."

Zac had been tempted to ask Pheobe about Tillie, but he was anxious to get to the mine and didn't wish to begin any long conversations. But now he posed the question to Lem.

"When I left Lem, you were pretty much convinced that Tillie was your daughter, sold away from you as a child. You were hoping the boy would show up. Tillie's brother. I've forgotten his name."

"Grafton. He be called Grafton. Took da most of da year after Tillie come to us but eventually, he showed up. Grievous bad hurt in dat war.

"Come a limp'n 'n' a-lean'n' on a stick, when he finally come. Told us da army doctor was guin cut da leg off. Grafton, he say no. So dey jest turned him loose, said he was on his own. Took all da next year to heal up some. He mos'ly a'right now. Cain't do no heavy work though, fer da pain.

"We's bought him a fine clothing store down ta da town. Man what raised him be a tailor and a clothing man. Grafton, he learn a lot from dat man. Doin' a'rite now. Good boy."

"Does he remember the old days, his childhood? Do you see anything of yourself in him?"

"Zac, dat boy looks like God made da two of us. Both from da same mold. Grafton 'n' me. Ain't no doubt to me. Grafton and Tillie be our little Grafton and Cecilia. No, sir. Jest ain't no doubt about it. Dey be our stolen an sold off chil'n."

If Lem had been smiling any wider he might have never pulled his face back into its normal shape.

Many questions were running through Claire's mind, but she knew this was not the time. She would hear the story later.

Zac stood to his feet.

"I'd like to see the mine. Can you guide us through?"

"Sure as ya know, I kin. Da lady want'n ta come too?"

Claire stood beside Zac.

"I wouldn't miss it for the world."

As they were making their way to the mine face, Zac asked, "Where's Dominik these days?"

Lem belted out a loud guffaw.

"Dat man, he ever'where. I do believe he may-be tap'd on ever rock on dis here mountainside.

Staked bunch a claims since y'all left. Ever one show'n promise. Da engineers, dey foller'n af'er him jest a breakn' chunks off fer da assayer. Dat dere Dominik, he be one gold hunt'n man. Nev'r know where at he might be till af'er he already bin der. He come to here by'n by."

Zac was amazed by the work done in the old mine. All four showings that Dominik had assayed before Zac left, plus the promising find that Zac, himself had discovered, had been opened. The rocky hillside was virtually riddled with shafts and interconnecting tunnels.

Zac considered the hours of back breaking work that had gone into the original small tunnel and shook his head in comparison.

He asked Lem about the constant draft he felt as they walked along.

"Oh, dat be da fans. Up on da rock, jest back a ways, t'wards da forest, fer ta get da wood, der be a big 'ol steam engine. Kep' a runn'n by four black mans da engineer train fer da job. Two on da days 'n' two others on da nights. I's tell da engineer, way back, dat we's goi'n make mor'n shovel men out'n da black workers.

"Steam, it be used for pull'n da ore carts up da slopes inside da mine. Used fer to run da steam drills ta make da holes fer da powder man. Used ta turn da big fans ta keep fresh air a mov'n along da tunnel."

Zac listened and nodded. He had heard about such things but had never seen it before. Again, he compared this to how they had so often worked in foul air as the original tunnel was deepened.

The lighting was still not so good though. Steam wasn't going to solve that problem. He wondered what would.

Claire was taking in every sight and sound. She

had never had any idea how a mine looked from the inside. It was a sight of wonder to her.

It seemed that they walked for miles, but of course it was really much less. The interconnecting tunnels, the slopes, the vertical shafts following the quartz trails, the pounding of the big steam drills, the shouts of men pushing carts, it was all a remarkable and wondrous sight to a ranch raised girl.

As they neared a newly blown face, Lem motioned for the other two to stop and wait. He stepped forward, raised one big hand, indicating that a shovel man should hold up a moment. He kicked a few larger rocks aside, bent and shuffled his hands through the smaller jagged rocks, and found what he was looking for. He picked up a fist sized rock and two much smaller ones. He rolled them in his hands, nodded in satisfaction, and stood. He carried the smaller ones to Claire. He passed the large chunk to Zac.

"Not enough light in here fer ta see real good. You take it inta da sun, you see what we bin work'n fer."

Lem led the two visitors to the entry door. Stepping into the light, they were all momentarily blinded as their eyes adjusted from the dimness.

Zac held the large chunk of ore. Claire was holding the two smaller ones, anxious to examine them more closely. A shout from a man pushing an ore cart forced them to step aside.

Lem stood smiling, watching Claire and waiting for a reaction. She rolled the two samples over and over in her hands, and then rolled them again. Finally, she lifted her eyes to Lem.

"Is this... Is this what I think it is? It can't be. Surely not."

"Yas, Mam, dat be zactly what y'all think it is. Dat der be gold, Mam, stick'n outa da white rock. Dat white rock be quartz. Dat what da min'n be all about."

"Why, why, it's beautiful. Like perfect jewelry. The most beautiful jewelry I've ever seen."

"Yas, Ma'am, dat sur enough be lac da jewelry. Lac maybe, God's jewellery.

"Down ta da big mill, dey crush da rock, 'n' separate da gold from da quartz. Den dey melt down da gold and form it inta nice bars fer ta sell. Dat what mak'n da min'n be profitable."

Zac was studying the larger chunk of mixed quartz, base rock and gold. Between the three pieces of rock Lem had picked up, there were several dollars worth of gold.

"Can someone place a value on these pieces? I'd like if we could keep them. Take them with us."

"We's jes goi'n have Tillie make da note in da records. You an owner. No one goi'n complain if'n you take da small bit a da ore."

A shrill blast from a steam whistle drowned out the talk. The mining noise gradually stopped as the drilling ceased. Dusty, tired men started walking out of the mine. Beside the office was a crew building where spare clothing and other supplies were kept. Attached on the sunny side of the building was a wash shack. Some men went to wash their hands and faces. Most headed directly for their lunch buckets. At least half of the workers were black.

Most of the men ignored Lem and Zac but to a man, they cast their eyes on Claire. She was uncomfortable with the attention, but she said nothing, knowing the men were little more than curious. Their need for food would soon have them looking the other way.

Zac, knowing that Lem had work to do, made their excuses and thanked him for the tour. They stepped into their saddles and waved farewell, heading back to town.

The first half of the ride was taken in silence, each sorting out their own thoughts. Claire's mind was still focused on the quantities of gold being dug from the hillside. She was totally at a loss to sort it all out. All she'd ever known was life on a Texas cattle ranch.

Of course, she had long understood that great wealth was being created in the newly worked West but to be face to face with it was causing her head to spin just a bit.

Nearing the town limits Claire said, "And you own a part of that operation?"

Without looking at her he answered, "Six percent. Sold the rest off to the big company."

"Six percent. Of an active prosperous gold mine! Six percent!"

Zac had nothing to add. The silence dragged on as they rode down Idaho Spring's main road, heading for the lawyer's office.

"Six percent of all that gold is yours?"

"Six point something. Not exactly sure what."

"Six percent and you're not sure what? That's just a bit casual Mister Trimble. I'd think you'd want to know the exact number."

A few seconds went by before Claire said, "Six and some percent of a gold mine and you're risking your life and limb chasing stolen cattle for total strangers. Riding over half of the west with a woman you don't even know. Have I got that about right?"

Zac didn't bother to respond.

Claire chose to let it drop for the time being.

CHAPTER TWENTY-FOUR

At the lawyer's office Zac and Claire dismounted and tied their animals. As Zac reached for the door, a ruddy faced, corpulent man, pulled it open from the inside and stepped into the opening, nearly bowling Zac over in his rush. Zac stepped back to give him room.

"S'cus me," the man offered. Then he noticed Claire and automatically reached for his hat. Just a slight tip of the front brim was offered and then he was past. Pulling a kerchief from his jacket pocket, he wiped his sweating face and hurried down the boardwalk.

Zac and Claire walked through the doorway left open in front of them. While Zac was closing the door, Claire nodded to Gomer. She was crossing the small office to greet Tillie. A quick 'hello', and then she knelt and spoke to the baby.

"Well hi there again, baby Sarah. How are you this afternoon?"

The baby, old enough to stand, holding the corner of the desk but not yet walking, took her thumb from her mouth and reached for her mother's flowing skirt, seeking refuge.

Claire rose to her feet, still smiling at the child. Without a word, she laid a small piece of gold laden quartz on the desk in front of Tillie. Tillie picked it up and rolled it in her fingers.

"Beautiful isn't it? Did Dad give you this?"

"Yes. In fact, he gave me two like that."

She lifted the second piece from her jacket pocket and passed it to Tillie.

"He gave a larger piece to Zac. We offered to buy them, but he said that you would make a note in the records and that would be the end of the matter. I can see that for Zac, as a shareholder, but I'm not a shareholder. I'm perfectly willing to purchase them both. I would have them mounted as pins or broaches. They're jewellery rock in my opinion."

Tillie gathered the two pieces together and pushed them towards Claire.

"Keep them and welcome. I'll make the note in the file.

"Now, tell me what you've been up to. Obviously, you were at the mine. Did Dad take you through the workings?"

"He did. I was totally fascinated."

Claire pulled a chair across the tiny office and up to Tillie's desk. Sitting down, she said, "I wouldn't want to work in a mine, but the tour was certainly eye opening."

"I agree," said Tillie. "I've been through it a couple of times. That's enough for me."

Zac showed the larger rock to Gomer, who expressed little interest. He then laid it on Tillie's desk. She didn't show much more interest. She simply said, "Nice," and pushed it back to Zac.

Curious, Zac asked, "Who was the out of breath gent we met in the doorway? I don't recall seeing him before."

Gomer laughed. Shaking his head, he answered, "That's the mining company's runner, although I can't somehow picture him doing much running. He carries the reports from the mine and the mill. Brings them here for Tillie to record. Does it every day. Good guy. Very serious about his work. He does the same for several mines. Somehow created a job out of such a simple thing."

Gomer laid down his pen, stood and stretched, and said, "Past lunch time."

That was the signal for Tillie to put her pencil down and reach for the baby. Standing and cuddling the baby in her arms, she said simply, "I'm ready."

Settled into the little café, Claire held her hands out to the baby.

"Pretty Sarah, how would you like to come and sit with me? We could get to know each other a bit."

The baby reached for her mother, but Tillie took her hand and laid it in Claire's outstretched hand.

"It's alright, Sweetie, you can go to the lady."

It took a few more minutes to break down the baby's suspicions, but finally she was sitting on Claire's knee. Claire smiled and looked at Sarah as she talked to Tillie.

"I don't really know much about babies. Never had many around the ranch. This one's a keeper though, I can easily see that."

Claire cuddled the baby while she ate with one hand. The other three at the table were talking mining and business, profits and expenses. The meeting went on until Tillie finally said, "I think it's time I changed and fed Sarah. I'll slip back to the office. Y'all come along when you're done up here."

Back at the office later, Zac spoke to Claire.

"You're welcome to hang on here if you wish but you might find the mining talk a bit boring. Gomer and Tillie are going to bring me up to date on the past two years and where the company sits now.

"Missus Templeton would welcome you to her veranda. She keeps an ever-filled pitcher of lemonade that's always at the ready. You suit yourself. I'm going to unsaddle my horse and let him graze a bit in the shade at the side of the building."

Claire stood and thanked Gomer and Tillie for the visit.

"I believe I'll be leaving you. That veranda sounds enticing. I may even feel a nap coming on."

CHAPTER TWENTY-FIVE

When Claire awoke from her nap and walked out to the veranda, she found Mrs. Templeton visiting with Phoebe. As promised, the lemonade pitcher was sitting in the shade and the glasses were ready for the taking.

The conversation soon got around to Zac and the trip west. Claire could easily see that Phoebe and Lem held Zac in high esteem. As Phoebe told portions of the story that Zac had not mentioned, Claire began to understand that the esteem came partly because of how he had always treated the black couple, even before the war. He had never showed any disrespect towards them and when it was time to escape Texas, he treated them as equals the entire time.

Claire finally got the stories of Phoebe's kidnapping and Zac's rescue, as well as the tale of Zac's wounded hip. But even then, she wondered if all the details had been included.

They skirted around the matter of Zac's depression and mood swings, respecting that much of his privacy.

Mrs. Templeton offered only, "Awful, terrible is

war. I do believe Phoebe, that young Grafton may be showing a little bit of what ails Zac, only not near so bad."

Phoebe only nodded silently in agreement.

The big hotel dinner was a joyous celebration reuniting old friends, old business partners. They managed to laugh about how hard they had worked that first year and how close they were to being broke before they mined enough gold to keep going. The men were vociferous in their praise of Phoebe who had kept them all fed and cared for in the big tent.

During a lull in the conversation Claire turned her head towards Dominik, who was seated a bit away from her.

"How did you meet up with these folks, Dominik? I don't believe I've heard anything about that."

Dominik told the much-shortened story of his travels from Poland and how he had found a small gold strike just as he had spent his last dime.

"I was very hungry. I could do no more work without food. I caught a racoon. I cooked it and tried to eat it."

Everyone at the table burst into laughter at the remembrance of the old story.

"God not put racoon on earth for to eat.

"I walk to town. I beg for food from small eating house. Lady say no, too many hungry, she no can feed all. I was close to crying with hunger. This man, Zac, he call me to the table. He tell girl to bring me food."

He pointed to Zac and Lem and Phoebe.

"These people. They save my life. I show them my mine. We become partners. We work very hard. Now you see mine. Is goot, no?"

Claire said, "Yes, I would say it is good. Very good."

Zac was pleasantly surprised at how Dominik had grown in his use of English. His Polish wife, Bianka was using the language effectively too, but with a much broader accent.

Bianka and Tillie were sitting side by side. Their little girls, Sarah and Zofia laughed and giggled together throughout the meal.

Lem and Phoebe's son, Grafton joined the group but had little to say.

The first day in Idaho Springs set the pattern for the next two days.

Claire alternated her hours between visiting and napping at the boarding house and exploring the town. She made a point of locating Grafton's clothing store. While he had been quiet at the dinner, he was welcoming and quite talkative, alone with Claire.

Zac spent most of his time at the mine or at the new sites Dominik had staked. By the end of the third day his head was spinning with visions of tunnels, equipment, fans, air vents, steam engines, steam drills, and all the other equipment it took to keep a modern mine operating.

Looking at Dominik's new claims, all filed in the name of the original owner's private company, that included only Dominik, Lem and Phoebe, as well as Zac, he came to believe that the future was bright indeed in the mining business.

Still, he didn't want any more of the work or the tension. He happily gave up a portion of the profits to the partners in return for his absence.

At dinner on the third day, Zac, believing he had accomplished all he set out to do, announced, "We'll be pulling out at first light in the morning. We've still got a herd to drive back to New Mexico."

CHAPTER TWENTY-SIX

With the guidance of the sheriff and some additional information gained from the livery hostler, Zac and Claire managed to locate a trail that would avoid Georgetown and still get them to where the cattle had been left grazing. That the new trail wound through the hills in an almost random fashion, with several false leads heading into starvation holes, didn't bother Zac. He was good on a trail, seemingly able to sense directions even in full darkness or on a cloud shrouded day.

He conceded to himself that he wasn't as good at finding hoof marks as Trig had proven to be. But he wasn't about to get lost. He was confident that he could sort it all out. Finding the crew and the cattle was only a matter of time.

The more direct route they rode on the way to Georgetown had been covered in a single day. This new, less direct trail turned the return ride into a full two-day trip. But after everything that happened in Georgetown, Zac felt it would be best to avoid the place.

Even after the many nights on the long trail from Texas, Claire was still just a bit nervous when the sun bid farewell to the land. She sometimes found herself imagining all types of threats, from bears to wolves to two legged varmints on the prowl.

During their ride north in search of the cattle trail, she was considerably comforted by the presence of three fighting men. Of course, she could do her own share of fighting, if it came to that.

By agreement, there was always one of them on watch.

Now there was just herself and Zac. It was certainly true that Zac had proven himself when challenged, whether at his own ranch on that first stormy evening or at the slaughterhouse in Georgetown.

And then there was the startling story of Zac's heroism in Idaho Springs that Phoebe recited during their visits.

Unquestionably, Zac was a competent guide and a watchful man around a camp or trail. She had no choice but to trust him for her safety, even thought there was now just the two of them.

Zac had stressed that he was a light sleeper, which was good because Claire, herself, either lay in her bedroll imagining all kinds of troubling possibilities. Or she slept like a rock. There was no middle ground.

It would be good to rejoin the group.

Their first day out of Idaho Springs found them preparing an evening meal in a little cirque created by the re-routing of a small stream. With the hundreds of men panning every stream in sight, often digging down to bedrock in their search for gold, many streams had been diverted.

With green grass for the horses pushing up through the wounded, tree cleared land, and water for coffee and washing up, the cirque was perfect for their needs.

After a simple meal and with the coffee made, Zac brought a pan of water from the stream and put the fire out. The resultant darkness took Claire by surprise.

"It's dark without the fire. I guess I wasn't paying enough attention to the lateness of the afternoon."

"That's why I put it out. The fire would be like a beacon to anyone following, or even just happening along. I'm not figuring on welcoming visitors tonight. Your eyes will adjust in a short while.

"On the trail in more dangerous circumstances, you'd be wise to keep your eyes away from the brightness of the flame."

When Zac began dismantling the camp, putting everything back in the packs, Claire joined him. They were soon ready to move on.

"We'll push along now to another spot before we settle down for the night."

Zac picked up the reins of both horses and held them while Claire mounted. He then wrapped the hot coffee pot in a blanket and passed it up to her.

"If you can handle this it would be a help. We'll be wanting another cup."

With barely enough light to see, Zac walked the horses along the trail until he spotted an opening in the aspens that bordered the narrow walkway. He wordlessly led the way in.

"We'll make as little noise as possible from now till morning. And we'll have no fire. You set the pot where we can get at it. I'll stake out the animals. Might be a bit of graze here and there."

He dropped the packs on the ground and then the saddles. Within minutes, he was back from caring for the animals. He immediately reached for his bedroll. Quietly he explained, "I'll lie here between the trail and wherever you decide to roll out your gear."

A half hour later, with the coffee pot empty and rinsed out, they were about to settle down for the night.

Claire spread her bedroll out and sat on it. She looked around their camp site, seeing nothing but bare outlines of trees in the darkness of the night. She looked towards where Zac had laid out his blankets. She hesitated, and then quietly spoke.

"Zac. You have been nothing but a gentleman on this trip. I need to thank you for that. A year ago, I wouldn't have dreamed of traveling alone with just one man. The trip west with Trig was a challenge to the conventional system, I guess. Certainly, my parents were horrified by the very idea. But we were travelling as part of a large group, so I pushed my concerns aside.

"It was much the same riding with you three men seeking the cattle. Safety in numbers was my thought. But now we're alone. I need to thank you for being a gentleman."

She left her thoughts there.

Zac couldn't think of a single reasonable response, so he went to check the horses one last time.

The next morning, they rose in full darkness and were on the trail well before first light. Zac had suggested that they could stop after the sun was up to build a breakfast fire.

The narrowness of the brush lined trail meant they could either ride one behind the other, or, if they doubled up, they would be riding almost knee to knee. Claire made the decision to pull level with Zac. There was something she wanted to ask about. If she could only find a way to start the conversation.

After a couple of hesitant and then discarded ideas, Claire glanced sideways at her riding partner.

"You stop me if you wish, Zac, but I've been wondering."

When Zac said nothing, she continued.

"Anna and I come from a believing family. Church attendance and private worship were always important. I'm normally content to leave folks to their own beliefs, but I couldn't help hearing you tell that banker fella to make out a draft for a Reverend Moody, I believe it was."

"Moody Tomlinson," was all Zac said in response.

Claire allowed a bit of silence to pass by before she continued.

"I take it he was a minister in your hometown. He must have been a friend to send him so much money."

Claire left the conversation there, hoping Zac would explain.

He did explain, but only briefly and not until he had chewed on it for a full minute.

"Moody's a good man. I've known him for many years. My family attended his church. When I came home from the war, I found them buried in the church yard there.

"The last thing he said to me before I lit out was, 'Is it still well with your soul?'"

Claire waited, but when no more was said, she asked, "Well, is it still well with your soul?"

Zac looked at her for the first time since the conversation began. He took several deep breaths and chewed his bottom lip.

"That question sometimes wakes me up at night and comes to me in the heat of the day. And I don't know. I just don't know. There's been so much..."

When Zac nudged the gelding into a slow trot Claire let him go.

By late-afternoon, after backtracking twice from false trails, they rode into the walled-up acreage where the herd had been held. The makeshift gates were down and left open. There was no sign of cattle. The shack was empty when they rode into the yard.

Zac looked at the sun.

"Getting late so we have a choice. We can settle down for the night in the shack or we can ride a couple more hours. I don't expect the crew will have driven the cattle too far. They had to gather them all up. Push them out of the brush and forest. Then, they were going to hold up a couple of days before they started. Give them some time to graze this fresh grass. Full stomachs might make the animals easier to handle. Lots of miles to cover.

"We might be just one day catching up or it could be two or three. Shouldn't be more. It's your choice. Stay in the cabin or move on a few more miles."

Claire stepped to the ground in front of the cabin. She tied her horse at the rail and entered the building. After a quick look around, she turned back to Zac who was standing beside his horse, waiting for her decision.

"I'm thinking we could benefit from a better sleep on these bunks, as poor as they are. So far, I haven't been able to find any ground that a person would really call soft. Don't expect it'll get any better either. And then, cooking on a stove, even just a sheet iron stove, is better than an open fire. I'm for taking what's before us."

Zac tied his horse and pulled his pack and bedroll off. He entered the cabin, chose a bunk and dropped the pack. Within a couple of minutes, he had done the same with Claire's pack. The saddles were brought inside, safe against possible rain. The horses were watered and tethered out. By that time Claire had a fire going in the little sheet iron stove and was digging around for provisions and utensils.

Zac walked outside, searching the bush all around the clearing. Claire wondered what he was doing but, on his return, he chose to say nothing. She put it down to his never-ending cautious nature.

A night in the shack and two more long days in the saddle had them well along the south trail. With the churned-up grass and the still wet droppings it wasn't difficult to follow, but the crew had made better time with the herd than they had first thought.

They took a side trip into Fairplay to re-provision, then got right back to riding, without further delay.

The first sign of the drive was the dust cloud in the distance. The westerly winds, dropping down from the high-up hills was causing the dust to float off to the east. Zac led the way to the less dusty side of the herd.

The first rider they caught up to was one of the hired hands. Half asleep in the saddle, he was startled into full wakefulness when Zac spoke to him. He was so close he could have reached over and touched the man. Zac remembered his name as 'Smiley'.

"Three critters have dropped off, back a ways, Smiley. Best you ride back, dig them out of those rocks and bring them along."

Smiley lifted his head in shock, looked at the herd and then turned to see Zac. It took a few moments to get his mind back into focus. Finally, recognizing Zac, he wiped his face with his rope burned hand and then readjusted his hat. With a shake of his head he let out a puff of held breath.

"Whew. Dozed off. Can't deny that. Long trail, and hot.

"That sure enough true? What you said? Three critters dropped out? Didn't think I was gone that long."

Without waiting for an answer Smiley wheeled his horse and rode back to the rocky upthrusts a quarter mile back. Zac immediately swung towards the herd, forcing a few more stragglers into the bunch.

When Smiley returned, pushing the three strays ahead of him, Zac and Claire rode forward. Smiley offered a small wave and a tip of his hat as they rode past.

CHAPTER TWENTY-SEVEN

The larger group of riders was brought back together with the arrival of Zac and Claire. Sitting together at the dinner fire that evening, they caught each other up on their doings.

Zac looked over at Randy, who seemed to be the leader of the Texas cowboys.

"You boys still alright? Can we depend on you till the trail is done?"

Randy spoke for his group. The other three had ridden out after dinner, taking their turn with the herd. Privately the men had discussed the matter just that afternoon, after the arrival of Zac and Claire, so Randy had a ready answer.

"We'll stick. Just so's y'all keep headin' south, we'll stick. South and east is home, and we're gett'n closer with every step these brutes take. Besides all that, we're broke and need'n the pay. Ya, we'll stick."

Several days later the herd was crossing a wide, grassy, high country plain. As was usual in the area, rocky upthrusts and rough terrain cut the grasslands, here and there. There were no large bodies of water, but numerous small watercourses were sufficient to keep the animals satisfied.

To keep her out of the worst of the dust, and because the trail and the riding were easy, Claire had been assigned the point position. It was her job to ride ahead, figuring the best way through the broken country and providing someone for the herd to follow.

In a rougher, nervous, Longhorn herd, she would not have been there. But the crossbreds of the WO were a more stable animal, and much less given to being frightened into a run. Still, she stayed far enough ahead to give her time to escape to the side in the event of a stampede.

Leonard and Trig were riding the swing positions, Leonard on the west side and Trig on the east.

When three riders were seen approaching from the west, Claire stopped, turned her horse sideways on the trail and looked back at Leonard. Leonard lifted his horse into an easy lope, closing in on Claire. Together they moved out of the way of the drive and sat waiting as the three riders approached. They both pulled their carbines, holding them across their laps.

While still out of comfortable shooting range the riders pulled up. A broad-shouldered man riding one of the biggest horses Leonard had ever seen motioned for his two companions to hold up while he rode forward with his right hand raised, palm out. Leonard took his actions as a sign of peace.

Showing no particular concern, but trotting up from his flanker position, Zac, as always, had the Henry held almost out of sight, along his right leg.

The approaching rider closed within hailing distance. With a lift of his hat he walked his horse forward.

"Just pass'n through, folks?"

Leonard spoke for the crew.

"Exactly so. Don't figure on stopping, beyond some rest time, this side of Santa Fe."

The men looked each other over for some time before the visiting rider turned his eyes to Claire and then to the herd. He looked longest at the approaching Zac. He spoke to Leonard while he looked over the red animals.

"Lot's of country here, folks, but it's pretty much spoken for. Little more room south a ways and over west but right here's taken. Now, I heard what y'all said. I'm just mak'n it clear."

Leonard took another look at the man. Not tall. Certainly not handsome. Totally bald, as he'd seen when the man lifted his hat. Broad and thick in the body and shoulders. Looked tough as saddle leather. Might be a poor man to make an enemy of.

"I'll say it again, stranger. We have no intention of stopping this side of Santa Fe. We're not after your grass, or anyone else's either. Just pass'n through."

After the rider completed his inspection of the situation, he lifted his hat again, just a bit, nodding slightly towards Claire.

"Names Luke. Luke Black. Came west with some folks nigh onto two years ago. They settled a bit to the north and east. Mac and Margo McTavish. You might have come past their Bar-M.

"I staked some holdings just west a bit. Them's my riders wait'n up yonder. Mex's. Good men. Don't know much English but good riders. Good fighters too."

Luke never really meant to be aggressive. It just seemed to be a part of his life. His nature.

Zac had arrived in time to hear this last bit. He didn't care for the attitude shown.

"Friend, I believe you've been told. We don't want your grass and we offer no threat to you or what's yours. Now, if you've finished with your talk we'll just keep moving along. If there's more you wish to say, spit it out. We need to make some miles. Ain't no intention of stopping here nor anywhere else till nighttime catches up with us."

Leonard had waved for the riders to keep the herd moving.

Luke settled back down into his saddle and let out a breath.

"Didn't mean to come across hard, folks. Gotten to be a habit, I guess. This can be a hard country. Sometimes we've got to be just as hard to hold it. Good country, though. Been a few along here studying the grass. I'm short of cattle to hold the range, in the eyes of some. Still, I'll have no one take what I've staked out. I'll have animals enough just as soon as I can find some to buy."

He took another long look at the passing herd.

"Any chance these here could be bought? Good looking animals. And I'm surely in the market."

Leonard answered again.

"Sorry. These are WO animals from down in the Agua Fria country. Stolen some time back. Found them up in gold country, what was left of them. No, I believe we'll just take them on home."

Luke showed his first hint of a smile.

"Sorry about that. Good look'n animals, he repeated. You hear of anyone that wants to sell, you send them my way. I'm look'n to buy maybe up to five thousand head. I want good animals though. Money's sett'n in a Denver bank not doin' me, nor anyone else any good."

Leonard closed out the visiting time, anxious to get back to the herd that had now passed them by.

"I hear of any animals available I'll remember that. For now, we've got work to do."

Luke nodded and again tipped his hat to Claire.

"You surely do. A good many miles to Santa Fe. Don't know this Agua Fria you mention. Ride safe, friends."

Zac jumped in with a question.

"Rode down this way a couple of years ago. Met a fella named Jimbo. Interesting sort of dude. Almost looked part Indian. You ever see him around?"

Luke pushed his hat back and slapped his knee. Grinning, he said, "That old reprobate's the one that guided us to this high-country valley. Great friend to Mac and Margo, up to the Bar-M. I do believe he's ridden about every mile of this here West. Sure enough, I know him. Good man in his way. Undependable though. He just might saddle up and ride off for months at a time, right when you needed him. Unpredictable. Ain't seen him for a spell. Zac is your name? I'll tell him you left a 'hello' next time I see him."

He swung his horse and loped up to where his riders sat waiting. Within half a minute they were out of sight, down a rocky draw.

CHAPTER TWENTY-EIGHT

The herd was nearly another week getting to the little sheep spread where the crew had stopped on the trip north. A full week after that they were nearing the WO range. With no extra mounts, the drive was kept to a slower pace than normal, the days shorter.

Leonard and Claire turned off for Santa Fe, leaving Zac in charge of the last few miles. Claire was certain Walter would still be under the doctor's care and that Anna would be there with him.

Trig watched them ride off, not knowing that Zac was studying him the whole while. Trig turned back to see Zac get the last of a knowing grin off his face. Trig hunched his shoulders and returned the grin.

"Rode all those hundreds of miles across Texas with her. Just concerned about her well being, is all."

Zac nodded his head while the grin returned.

"Ya. Concern. That's what I saw. Concern."

"Well, I suspect you're not quite as dead to feelings as you make out, neither, old friend. Ain't none of us completely immune to a beautiful woman."

Zac nodded and turned to the herd again, having had enough of the conversation. Any more talk and who knew what either one may say in a weak moment.

"Let's get these animals to home."

Claire and Leonard tied their horses to the picket fence in front of the doctor's office and walked up to the door. The doctor pulled the door open just as they got there. He was carrying his black bag and appeared to be in a hurry. He took a quick glance at his visitors and said, "They ain't here no more. I did what I could, short of tying that man to the bed. He was bound and determined to get out to the ranch. Been gone near a week now."

With that he scurried around the house towards his buggy and the one-horse shed beside it.

CHAPTER TWENTY-NINE

It was late afternoon when the WO cattle were pushed onto their home range, spreading out over the many acres of the Agua Fria grasslands. Anna stood on the top step looking in wonder at the sight before her. Walter, still convalescing, sat in a large wicker chair on the veranda, with a blanket wrapped around his chest and shoulders. His wounded leg was propped up on a padded stool. Neither had words to describe either their feelings or the sight before them.

Being an experienced ranch woman, Anna finally tore her eyes off the men and cattle and turned to the door. She made her way quickly to the kitchen. She stoked the stove, put a couple of sticks of split wood on the coals and refilled the coffee pot. She had taken a count of the men driving the herd. She would need both of her large frying pans to prepare enough food to satisfy a crew of that size.

Leaving the stove long enough for it to heat up, she again took up a post on the top step. The sight of the field populated with red cattle filled her with thankfulness and wonder. She had no knowledge yet of where the animals had been driven to or how many were left. But clearly, the cowboys had done a wonderful job.

Then she re-thought. Of course, it would be Claire and the cowboys. But where was Claire? She wasn't with the herd or with the men, who were now making their way into the ranch yard. And where was Leonard? The wanting to know was testing her patience.

She finally turned to Walter, wiping a tear from her cheek.

"Have you ever seen anything so wonderful? I can't imagine what all has happened in the weeks they've been gone."

Walter didn't try to stand, although he wanted to. The doctor had been very clear, and Walter had agreed to heed the instructions: a slow careful walk to the veranda or the outhouse, with help close by. Nothing more.

Still, how can a man sit through such an event? He squirmed at the anticipation of greeting the men and hearing the story but resisted the temptation to push himself to his feet.

The men dismounted at the small barn. After pulling the saddles and bridles, they turned their horses into the empty corral and followed them in to see to the water and feed.

With that done, Zac and Trig made their way to the house, while the four hired riders hung around the shade of the barn.

Anna could no longer hold back her feelings. She rushed down the stairs, crossed the small yard, swung open the gate and moved towards the two men; the same two men who were total strangers not long before. But even in her rush, her mind detailed off the enormous impact these men had on their lives and the life of the WO.

First, she gave Zac a firm hug and then turned to Trig. Neither man lifted an arm to return the expression. When Anna finally stepped back, tears brimming, Zac tipped the brim of his hat.

"Glad to be back, Ma'am."

Trig lifted his hat off and held it in his two hands.

"Good to see you, Ma'am. Looks like Walter is up and about."

Anna turned glassy eyes towards the veranda.

"Well, up anyway. Not so much about. But we're both pleased at how he's healing. And, oh my, I can't express how happy I am to see you. You and the cattle too. But where are Claire and Leonard?"

With a grin Trig said, "Why, Ma'am, they're off to Santa Fe, visiting y'all, see'n to your welfare."

Anna grinned back at Trig.

"I expect they'll figure it all out and we'll see them soon enough. But, oh, do come to the veranda and tell us all about it. And tell the riders there's a fresh pot of coffee coming real soon, and dinner will be ready shortly."

Walter and Anna listened in silence as Trig told the tale. Zac was being his normal quiet self. He listened for a few moments before leaving the story to Trig. He rose quietly from the veranda chair and made his way to the corral. Leading his gelding by a hold on the mane, he directed the animal to the small barn. In a stall that clearly hadn't been used for some time, he slipped a halter on the animal and secured it to the feed manger.

With a curry comb and a brush that were hanging from nails driven into a post, he treated the faithful animal to a thorough grooming. With that done, he led the gelding outside and turned it loose to graze the green grass of the ranch yard, knowing it wouldn't wander far.

The four Texas riders took turns with the comb and brush after Zac was done with it.

Zac was sensing the old feeling of hollowness. The emptiness that often came over him when a stressful job of work was put behind him. It was if he could finally relax. But relaxing too thoroughly might put him into the dreaded black hole.

He needed to be alone after the weeks of working closely with the others. He walked to a short section of rail fence overlooking the close-in pasture. With his arms folded across the top rail he pondered the recent past, and the near future. The sight of the field of red cattle again grazing their home range gave a comforting feeling of a job well done.

He knew that what he really should do is saddle up again and head for Las Vegas, and his Wayward Ranch. He had done what Claire had asked of him. He, and those who rode with him, had put on many a long mile, risking their lives in the doing. But he told himself, the job was done. And done well.

Certainly, in the narrow sense, that was correct. But there was a broader way to look at it also.

Who was really behind the rustling, the stealing of cattle? Who was Harold Zaborski's contact person, his supplier? He certainly couldn't engineer a steal such as was done on the WO without a southern accomplice. And then, what about the other rustling he had been told of?

Had the JJ Connected or the A-Bar given up on their rustled animals or did they still have riders searching the hills? Who else might have had their herds cut? Were all the animals driven north to the gold fields or were there other buyers in other locations?

And were there other Harold Zaborskis out there, feeding those other markets? Had there been other murders, as there was on the WO?

He had that one name, Gibbs, foreman of the Lazee ranch. But it was unlikely that a ranch foreman was the top dog in the scheme. So, who was the head thief?

And the biggest question of all was rattling around his conscience; Can I ride back to the Wayward Ranch and leave all those questions hanging?

Had not Trig stated it clearly, "Pa always advised that a job half done wasn't done at all?"

There's nothing urgent calling me back to the ranch. Perhaps I'll hang on for a while. Maybe take a ride south a ways. Find the JJ Connected or the A-Bar. Maybe take a look at the Lazee, but that's apparently a long ride.

Trig, being pretty much footloose, would probably want to ride along. Well, he's fair good company. Knew when to talk and when to keep his mouth shut. Didn't dig into the past and seems to know when to just let her lay. Pretty good hand with the coffee pot.

He figured Claire and Leonard would stay on the WO. Leonard had been anxious to get back to his Lincoln County ranch. But from the way he had been looking at Claire, Zac figured things might be changing.

That forced Zac to wonder again about his own feeling towards the woman. It was certainly true that he was often lonely. And Claire was an attractive, knowledgeable ranch-raised woman. A promising young woman who would be a great life partner for the right man. But was he the right man? Would it be fair to bring a good woman into his often troubled and convoluted world?

He craved long spells of aloneness. Seemed to need those times. They were a help in allowing his still war-damaged soul to heal. But aloneness was different from loneliness. And he admitted, only to himself, that he was sometimes lonely.

As he pondered, his mind seemed to flit and bounce from one subject to the next without his guidance, like a newborn colt, romping in the sun, just happy to be alive.

He raised his eyes from the cattle and took a long view of the surrounding hills. Somewhere in those hills lived a thief. A master thief. He could be disguised as a prosperous ranch owner or, as it was in Georgetown, a saloon owner, or some Santa Fe politician. It could be almost anyone. Whoever he was, he would eventually have to be found and stopped.

But was it Zac's job to find and stop the thief? Or Trig's? What about the law?

He knew and understood the situation with the law. In a country long settled by Mexicans but only recently infiltrated by newcomers, law was slow to develop. Most law was local. Town sheriffs didn't have time or assistants enough to police the whole area. Nor did they usually have legal jurisdiction. And the Mexican authorities largely left the new settlers to their own affairs.

Law in ranching country was often abrupt and final, administered by the ranchers themselves. Or by someone like Zac. Someone who said, 'This has to stop.'

CHAPTER THIRTY

Leonard and Claire rode into the yard late that evening. After the greetings were completed, they all settled down to rehash the recent few weeks and to have Claire fill in the parts of the adventure in Georgetown and Idaho Springs, that Trig and Leonard hadn't been a part of.

Zac again made his escape during the telling.

Claire was effusive in her praise of Zac, giving him full credit for the return of the cattle and for the bank draft that Anna had hidden away in a safe place. She was also generous with her telling of Trig's tracking abilities, as well as Leonard's steadiness and hard work.

She left out the part of her shooting the men outside the Georgetown saloon.

Claire, feeling that Zac's finances were his own private matter, said nothing at all about his ownership of the gold mine. She would leave that to Zac himself.

While the storytelling was going on, Zac made his way to the bunk house, where he had dropped his bedroll and saddle earlier. The four Texas riders were lounging around a rickety table, playing poker by the light of a smoked-up kerosene lamp.

He looked on for a few moments until he felt the time was acceptable for an interruption.

"Boys. You've been thanked for the work and for seeing it through to the end. I've got your pay here. You'll be paid a full month plus a bonus, even though the work is some shy of that amount of time.

"I'm expecting y'all might be planning on saddling up in the morning, hearing the call of the Texas winds, and all that. But here's something to consider.

"Walter has a job for each of you if you should be interested. The WO had just the two hands before all this happened. Two hands plus Walter himself. The ranch needs help, especially with Walter being laid up.

"I've got to be honest with you. Those two hands were both gunned down by the thieves that drove off the cattle."

He paused to allow that information to sink into the men's minds.

"We managed to break up the northern part of the rustling game, but we don't have any clear idea who's playing that same game down here. I intend to sort that out and see that it comes to an end.

"There's no reason to suspect the thieves will return to the WO, but there's also no guarantee that they won't. If you wish to stay on for a while, you'll face that risk. But I don't expect the situation is very much different from what you'd face back in Texas, or in any newly settled ranching country.

"You have your weapons back and have, so far, proved yourselves trustworthy. You think on the offer and let me know by morning."

Zac counted out the men's pay and then made his way back to the veranda. He laid the remaining coins on the table in front of Anna and Walter.

When Walter said, "What's all this?" Zac explained about the thousand held back at the bank, minus the pay and other expenses. With no further words, he took a seat and reached for the coffeepot.

Anna picked up the gold coins and held them like found treasure, her eyes glistening. She showed them again to Walter, as if he might have missed seeing them.

Walter took a deep breath, adjusted his position in the big chair and looked over at Zac and Trig.

"I have no real idea how to value your services, men. Your help goes beyond simply work for hire. We would happily return these coins to be split between the two of you if that would be sufficient. That and our undying gratitude."

Neither man answered right away.

Finally, Zac said, "Trig can speak for himself. For me, I'm just happy to see those animals eating their own grass. Whatever is left after paying off Trig, you use towards fixing up the WO."

Everyone looked towards Trig. Although he was usually not short of words, he still hesitated. After a time, he cleared his throat and grinned his familiar grin.

"I expect one day I'll be broke and cadging a meal here and there from some ranches as I'm passing through. Might show up here again, on the WO, feeling the need of a bunk and a couple of square meals. You never can tell. But for right now I've still got a coin or two.

"Anyway, the past weeks have given me a story to entertain my grandchildren with. Or someone else's grandchildren if I fail to rope a woman dumb enough to take up with me.

"No, Anna and Walter. You hang on to those few coins. Anyway, we never did take an accurate count of the animals, either those driven north, or the ones left on the WO. It could be you're still short. I expect it'll take a full round-up to know for sure. The coins will help fill out whatever gaps you find."

CHAPTER THIRTY-ONE

The next morning Zac and Trig rode into Santa Fe and found the sheriff having his breakfast in a small eating house They had left the ranch early so another cup of coffee would be welcome.

"Morn'n, Martin."

Martin Garcia motioned to the empty chairs around the square table.

"Sit yourselves down, men. Take a load off."

The two men took seats and, as if they had rehearsed it, they both tipped their hats back and placed their folded arms on the tabletop.

The sheriff shoveled in another bite of egg. He wiped a drip of yellow yoke from his chin, and grinned.

"Like 'em runny. Wife nearly gags just watch'n. Wong, over there, he sets 'em just right. The way I like them. Tak'n breakfast at Wong's allows for the wife to lay abed a while too. What kin I do fer ya? Heard ya got them WO animals back ta home."

Zac leaned back in his chair and grinned.

"Like my eggs a little runny myself. Can't quite manage them right from the shell though, like those seem to be. Tried often enough when I was a younker, stealing right from under the hen, eggs still warm.

"We got the animals alright. And the money to cover the costs of those that were already gone from the big bunch. Long ride. Clear to the gold fields. But now we want to find the thief on this end of the game. You mentioned two ranches that lost animals."

The sheriff nodded.

"JJ Connected and A-Bar."

"That's right. Up north we heard the name of another. The Lazee. Know anything about it?"

The sheriff leaned back in his chair and reached for the fixings. He carefully pulled a paper from the flat pack he lifted from his shirt pocket. A light tug on the string hanging from the same pocket lifted the Bull Durham pouch into his hand. He slowly spread the paper, creating a slight groove between two fingers, and carefully poured the tobacco. With the skill of long use, he folded and wrapped the paper around the tobacco. A lick to moisten and seal the paper, and a slight twist on each end completed the task.

He did all this without ever taking his eyes from Zac, except to glance towards Trig, just the one time. He fished in the other shirt pocket and came out with a match. A scratch on the underside of the table brought the wanted flame forth. A quick touch of the flame, a pull of breath, and the sheriff's mouth filled with smoke. He held it for a moment before sucking it into his lungs and then forcing it out through his nostrils.

"The Lazee, eh?"

The question needed no response.

"Guess most folks have heard of the Lazee. Big spread. Prosperous. Split up into three ranches, way I heard it. Two in New Mexico. One in Arizona. In the pine woods, so they tell.

"Owned by Bartholomeus Gantry. Big rancher. Big man. Big ideas. Deep pockets, I'm guessing. Came over the mountains from San Francisco some time back.

"Sometimes known as Major Gantry. Major of just what, I have no idea. Not a friendly man. Tough crew."

Zac leaned a bit closer.

"One of those crewmen named Gibbs?"

The sheriff slowly nodded.

"Mind telling us where this Lazee can be found?"

"Ain't never been there my own self. Heard is all. Closest I can come is just what I already told you. West of the J-J some ways, and then on into Arizona. West of here by quite a bit. Long ride. Best I can do, boys. Now I've got work to do."

Zac held out his hand to stop the sheriff from rising.

"JJ Connected and A-Bar?"

"Near Albuquerque. All I know."

Zac and Trig watched the sheriff cross the road. He seemed to have a weight on his back that was causing his shoulders to slump and his feet to drag.

Trig never peeled his eyes away from the sheriff's back. He spoke for the first time since entering the café.

"Never did enjoy the sight of a frightened man."

CHAPTER THIRTY-TWO

Zac and Trig had the blacksmith replace worn shoes on their horses while they went to the general store for traveling supplies. Zac spoke as they were slowly making their way around the store displays.

"You ain't exactly said. You buying for a ride south and west or you buying for a ride back to Texas?"

Trig grinned a bit.

"I'm gett'n kind of fond of this rid'n around, doin' not very much. Sure beats fix'n fences or rid'n rough stock. Course, a fella's like to get shot at from time to time. But life always seems to carry some challenges.

"Then, I figure if you and me could come back to the WO look'n like the heroes of the day one of us just might catch a certain young woman's eye. Never can tell. I mean, what's Leonard got to offer when you come right down to it? He slowly named off a few things, lifting a finger with each item.

"Alright, there's a solid family. Stable ranch. He's wealthy. Handsome. Dependable. Easy to get along with. Why those things don't amount to hardly noth'n at all.

"Compared to excitement and fun and great new

adventures, is what I mean. No, sir. Just noth'n at all."

Zac looked at the grinning young man across a counter piled high with checked shirts. He simply shook his head and held up a shirt, examining it for size.

By the next afternoon they were nearing Albuquerque.

Leonard had argued that he should be going along on the hunt. It was only when Walter said, "I need you here, little brother," that he finally relented. Still, he had watched Zac and Trig mounting up with a wistful look in his eye.

Claire also gave in to Anna's argument of needing help. But after the long ride from East Texas and then up to the gold fields and back, she too, was developing a bit of the wanderlust. Putting the WO back into working order was going to feel a bit dull after the past many weeks of travel.

As was Zac's habit, he rode first to the Albuquerque sheriff's office. The combined office and jail were attached to the village hall. In an effort to appear a bit more dignified than the average western town, the door had been lettered 'Slim Gadfry, Sheriff.'

After tying their animals, Trig pushed the door open and the two men entered. Behind the desk sat a large man, broad of girth and thick in the shoulders. His flat crowned hat added to the image of strength. He was the exact opposite of what the name 'Slim' conjured up.

Trig enquired, "Sheriff Gadfry?"

The big man was logically suspicious facing two armed men, although Zac had left the Henry in the saddle scabbard. Taking a hard study of the men, he slid his hand towards a Colt that was lying on the desktop.

"What can I do for you men?"

Zac stepped forward, holding out his hand.

"Zac Trimbell, Las Vegas. Work time to time with Link Spangler up that way. You ever met Link? Been sheriff there for some years now."

The sheriff glanced at the outstretched hand, then ignored it. Zac hunched his shoulders and pulled his hand back.

The still suspicious sheriff answered, "Heard of Spangler. Never met. Again, I ask, what can I do for you men?"

"Sheriff, this is Trig Mason. Riding for the WO ranch, up near Santa Fe. They had some rustling troubles. Couple of riders killed. Cattle driven north for beefing, up in the gold towns. We went and brought them back. As many as weren't already under the knife anyway."

Slim Gadfry had nothing to say, simply nodding as he listened.

Zac picked up the tale again.

"We'd kind of like to sort out the leader of the gang. Georgetown sheriff has the northern bunch safely under lock and key, but I'm not convinced any of them was really the top dog. Seems like the brains and the big money might be down this way. Or maybe just the southern sergeant, so to speak.

"With the telegraph strung all along the way, communication over distance is no real problem. We plan to check it all out. Might save some lives and a whole lot of theft and needless riding.

"Heard about a couple more thefts too. JJ Connected and A-Bar. Wondered what you could tell us about that."

"Can't tell you nothing at all. Wouldn't even if I could. Not real fond of vigilantes."

Zac turned to look at Trig, judging his response to the comment, and then turned back to the sheriff with a smile that had intimidated many a man.

"Well, Sheriff, it seems as how the thieves are still out there. Right here, in your jurisdiction. On the loose, you might say. At least the southern end of the thieving gang. Setting up to work their next big steal, I'm guessing. Maybe murder a rider or two. And here you sit. Could be, you might look kindly on some help, vigilantes or no. But have it your way."

Trig again held the door while Zac stepped back onto the sidewalk. Trig then followed, pulling the door closed behind himself.

They were just untying their reins from the hitch rail when the door opened. Sheriff Gadfry stepped out. He looked as if he had something to say, but as the men swung aboard their horses, he remained silent.

The next stop for enquiry was the livery stable. For all-around gossip and local lore there was no besting most livery men. They met travellers and heard stories. They kept their eyes on the town and their main entertainment was visiting and talking.

Trig remained mounted while Zac strolled into the big barn. He was met by a growling, but not unpleasant, voice coming from a box stall at the far end of the aisle.

"Howdy stranger. Be right with ya. Just gett'n the last of these desert burrs out'n the feathers on this big Clyde. Pure-de nuisance if ya was to ask me. Why the good lord put feathers on a horse has forever been a mystery to me. Why I've known horses that…"

Zac laughed, interrupting the talker.

"Don't stop your work on my account, friend. I'll just stroll down there to ask my questions."

"Ya. Questions. It's always questions. Gonna start charg'n for answers. Make more'n I do bent over brutes this big, combing out burrs that no way want to let loose."

Zac stepped down the aisle and leaned his folded

arms over the top plank on the stall gate.

"Now that is a beautiful horse. Does he have a mate? Seems like these Clyde's are usually running in pairs."

"Other one's out back, in the corral. In worse shape than this one when they brought him in. Took me a big part of the morn'n shoo'n 'em and gett'n 'em cleaned up. Wouldn't do it for just any-one. Friends. Good folks. Those that run the A. Do all their shoo'n and a bit of horse doctoring. What they can't do for themselves, is what I mean. Don't know as I'd do this for anyone else," he repeated.

"By the A, do you mean the A-Bar?"

"Yep, A-Bar. Most just call it the A. Best folks for many a mile around. Ol' Wishart, Noah Wishart, him that's dead these past many years. Started 'er all up back when there wasn't nothing but Mexi-cans and Indians through this whole area. Instead of fight'n and kill'n, he made friends with 'em. Not easy with the Indians, but he done 'er. Named the A after his wife, Abigale. Son Lucas, he runs 'er now. Good man too. Near as good a man as his old dad. What fer are ya askin?"

Zac didn't want his mission to become gossip throughout the town or the territory. He felt cau-tion was called for.

"Heard about them is all. Second hand. Coffee'd with a rider a while back. Talking kind of man. Mentioned the A. Passed on a bit of news that might be of interest to them. All friendly, I'll guarantee you that."

"Well, son, it ain't no secret. Where the ranch is, I mean. Anyone in town could guide you right. You ride west about ten miles on that red dirt track you'll see if'n you was to ride about a quarter mile south of here. Then take the trail off to the north. Might be a signpost at the junction. Not real sure about that. Used to be, some time back. Been a while since I was out that way.

"North trail leads towards a flat-topped mesa you'll see right there. Trail winds around some, but you stay with it. You'll find the A just a couple of miles beyond the mesa.

"If I thought you could be trusted with this team, I'd have you trail them along to the ranch. I've done up what needed doing. Save me the trip. Too many years hunkered over these brutes, shoe'n and pull'n burrs ott'n feathers that shouldn't aught ta be there in the first place. Back don't take ta rid'n so good no more. Be a help if'n you could be trusted with these here animals."

Zac wondered what level of trust would be needed to make such an enquiry of a stranger. Then, chuckling to himself he thought, 'These Clyde's will be a known team for miles around. Man would be a fool to try to run off with them.'

"You get them haltered with a good lead. I'll take them along. You don't know me, but you've got my personal guarantee that they'll arrive where you say. Names Zac Trimble. Wayward Ranch. Up near Las Vegas. Do some work with Sheriff Link Spangler from time to time."

"You a lawman?"

"Not regular. Link, he pins a deputy badge on me now and then. Those times he comes up with a two-man job. That's all."

The livery man wiped his hands on his pant legs and held one out for shaking.

"Pat. That's all anyone knows me by. Been called Pat ever since that one time… Well, never mind. That don't much matter anymore. I gotta learn ta let 'er go.

"Don't know this Spangler fella. Only been up that way the once. Lady I went to see greeted me kindly enough. We'd shared a couple of letters, 'n such. Figured the widow might make me a welcome. And she did. At first. Fed me a dinner to remember. Then she asks what it is that I work at. I told her plain. She curls her upper lip into a disapproval and ups and tells me she's not of a mind to live with the smell of horse forever in her home.

"That was some time back. Never saw no reason to go see the bright lights of Las Vegas again. Expect the widow's added a sight of misery to some other fella's life long before this date."

He looked up at Zac and grinned.

Pat led the Clydes down the wide barn aisle, a halter and a lengthy rope on each. He passed one lead to Zac and then reached up and gave the other one to Trig.

"Didn't know there was more than just the one of you."

Zac made the introduction before he asked one more question.

"The J-J out that same direction?"

Pat hesitated, carefully studying first Zac and then Trig. It was almost as if he was thinking out loud, tying the two ranches together in his mind. Looking for anything at all that might tie them together. Nothing came, at first. At least, nothing he wanted to talk about.

"Well, you could say the same direction. But you'd go on past the turnoff to the A and keep on a goi'n another ten miles or so."

He stopped his short speech when his mind finally got around to the rustling. That news had hit town like a cannon shot a good many weeks before. No one could figure who might have had the courage to drive off A-Bar animals.

Although good folks in most ways, the Wishart bunch wasn't known as easy. Or forgiving.

Before making friends with the Indians and the local Mexicans, Noah Wishart had been challenged many times. That he stood his ground with great valor, while remaining friendly, had impressed both hostile groups. With those actions he had gained a reputation for fairness and courage.

No. No one challenged the A and escaped unscathed.

Still, there had been no recent news about the losses, and the town folks were apt to have other things on their minds by then. Now these two, one at least a sometimes deputy, arrived in town asking questions.

Pat let his eyes fall to the ground as these thoughts ran through his mind. He wondered what these strangers might know. Did they know about the rustling? He decided to let it go. There may come a time but not yet.

Pat shook off these thoughts and looked back up at Zac.

"Interesting you should be asking about them two particular ranches. You bein' a lawman, is what I mean."

Zac lifted the reins and snugged the lead line around the horn.

"Keep it all to yourself Pat. The less said, the better."

Trig asked, "The sheriff ridden out that way recently Pat?"

Now Pat looked troubled. Without giving an answer to the question he said, "You ride careful now boys. And don't lose those Clydes along the way."

CHAPTER THIRTY-THREE

When Zac and Trig rode into the A-Bar ranch yard, there was a reception waiting. Two women, one older, one younger, stood on the house veranda. Three riders lounged before the cookhouse, picking their teeth after the noon meal. One man, probably the wrangler, walked slowly from the big barn, a coiled lariat in his hand. Two men stood in the center of the yard, one dressed like a typical working cowboy. The other with the prosperous appearance of a ranch owner about him. Both were armed with holstered Colts.

Zac spoke over his shoulder to Trig.

"Flat country once you're past that mesa. Expect we've been watched for a couple of miles."

As they rode past the barn and the corral, the man who had been approaching said, "Howdy."

Zac pulled up, unwound the lead from his saddle horn and passed it to the man. Trig did the same.

"Pat sends his greetings."

The wrangler looked the Clydes over quickly and then turned to Zac.

"Thanks. He does good work. They're look'n fine."

Zac lightly tickled the gelding into motion with

one spur and rode towards the two men standing in the yard. As was custom, they stayed mounted until they were invited to step down.

Zac lifted his hat just a bit.

"Zac Trimbell, Las Vegas. This is Trig Mason, new out from East Texas. I judge you're Lucas Wishart. Pat sends his greetings, along with them Clydes. I'm thinking he'd prefer if you could keep them out of the desert and away from the burrs in the future. He didn't just exactly say that. I'm just supposing."

The cowboy asked, "How is it that Pat sent those animals out with you. He know you? You're strangers to us."

Zac smiled at the man, feeling the belligerence the fella was trying to hide.

"We never met until three, four hours ago. I'm guessing he just took a shine to my honest face. That, and the fact that I sometimes deputy for the Las Vegas sheriff. Seems he felt he could trust us. He was right about that."

While Zac was answering the foreman, he was really talking to Lucas Wishart.

The A-Bar owner spoke up.

"Step down. The wrangler will care for your mounts. We'll go see if there's a slice of pie left to go with some coffee. This is my foreman, Bobby Cromwell."

When they were all on the ground the introductions were made again, this time with handshakes and words of welcome.

Seated, with coffee and pie before them, Zac told why they were there.

Lucas was a while responding. But finally, he said, "Heard about the rustling up Santa Fe way. And about the dead punchers. No details. Just that a large bunch had been run off. Hadn't heard about retrieving the animals. That's a story I might wish to hear in detail."

Trig said, "Hardly time for the story to get down this way. We only rode back onto the WO with the animals a few days ago."

Zac asked, "Do you mind telling us how many animals you lost and what they were; Longhorns, white face or?"

Buddy answered for the ranch.

"We shipped off the last Longhorn bull two years ago. Only white face bulls now. Longhorn look is getting bred out. Mostly solid red hides showing in the herd. Still some show of horns. Reckon that'll disappear bye 'n' bye too."

Lucas stepped into the silence that followed.

"Our herds are scattered over a wide territory. After the theft we did a field count, judging as best we could.

"Maybe close onto five hundred head missing."

"What have you done to find them?"

"Well, now, that's a problem."

Zac took the lead.

"Do you mind telling us about it? We're pretty determined to find the people behind the rustling of the WO stock. Two men are dead. Those rustled animals were in their care. Doesn't seem right to just let that go. Any lead would be a help."

The owner of the A-Bar took a long, hard study of his two visitors and seemed to come to a decision.

"It's a big, unsettled country here abouts, with a thousand gullies and canyons. Many of those gullies are barren of either water or grass but a few have both. I can't say that any of us has ever ridden the whole territory."

Lucas Wishart dressed and acted the part of a wealthy ranch owner. He was a big, well-fed man, thick in the shoulders, with a square jaw covered by a single day's growth of black whiskers. When he lifted his hat and laid it on the unused chair beside him, his long black hair flopped over his brow and down to his collar. Brushing his hair from his eyes and rubbing his chin were the parts of a single motion. The motion of a troubled man.

Zac, sitting across the table, could see the weariness in the man's eyes.

As if he was still wondering how far to trust these two visitors, Lucas studied the tabletop for several seconds before glancing back up at first Zac and then Trig.

Confirming his earlier decision, he turned toward his foreman.

"Buddy, I'm going to be here a while. I'd like if you could set out some work for the men. There's still a good part of the day left. Might as well make use of it."

Buddy glanced at his boss and then at Zac and Trig. As if his preference would be to stay and be a part of the conversation, he only slowly rose to his feet. He glanced back once, before pushing the cook house door open.

When he was gone, Lucas again rubbed his face. This time with both his hands. The stressed look could no longer be hidden. Zac had felt stress of that nature many times, sometimes self inflicted, by imagining things that would probably never happen, but also, often while seeking answers to seemingly unsolvable questions. Idly the thought ran through his mind, ranch troubles don't compare to being shot at, but troubles are troubles, I guess.

At the sound of crockery lunch plates being washed, back in the kitchen, Lucas turned on his chair and hollered out, "Rube, let it go for now. Go for a walk. Take a break. I'll let you know when we're done here."

When he was sure they were alone, Lucas stood and went for the coffee pot again. He re-filled all three of the thick, white mugs before setting the pot in the center of the table.

"Men, we live in troubled times. Most of it from the leftovers of the war.

"When Pa first drove a small herd into this country, he faced only two concerns. Of course, that's not including the weather. I mean two concerns he felt he could do something about. First there were the Mexicans who had been in the country for eons past. He solved that problem by loosing his herd where there was no sign of other settlement or range use.

"His second concern was the Indians, who hadn't yet figured out the white invaders. Of course, the white invaders hadn't figured out the Indians either. Pa thought it all through and got to wondering if any white settlers had bothered much with trying to figure out the Indians. Most, he decided, had tried to solve their problems with powder and lead.

"He knew, with the A-Bar being just him and ma and two little kids, two scared half-to-death riders and six hundred head of Longhorns, he couldn't fight those that were here first. That was a battle he was bound to lose."

Trig had listened to this introduction to the A-Bar story and couldn't hold back a comment.

"That sounds like smart thinking to me. Your Pa must have been a wise man."

Lucas took advantage of the break in the tale to gulp down some coffee, before answering.

"I guess you could call Pa wise. Or perhaps realistic. He and Ma were both young. Young and inexperienced in a new land. But they had talked it all through as best they could. They realized that a single foolish mistake could cost them everything.

"Pa first went to the local alcalde and had a talk. There was a language problem, but they worked their way through that with a few words of each other's language. That, and scratches in the dusty yard, outlining the area Pa meant to ranch in.

"Long story short, they ended the meeting with smiles and handshakes. Pa hired two young Mexican riders to seal the deal. One of those vaqueros taught me to ride. Good men, the both of them.

"Next came the Pueblos. There's a lot of other tribes in the area but the Pueblo were the ones right closest by. Fearing there was a good chance he might never return, Pa left instructions with Ma and the hired riders. He then rode off to negotiate a peace, driving two grown steers before him.

"Again, long story short. With the steers as a gift and several pouches of tobacco to spread around, Pa and the Pueblos, they made a peace. Of some sort anyway. But it's held over the years. Oh, there's been the odd couple of young bucks wishing to test their horse-stealing skills but it never amounted to much.

"Pa figured he had a pretty good idea who he could trust back in those days. He lived that way and it worked out for him. And for the family and the A-Bar. But things have changed.

"Except for that mess up at Glorieta Pass we pretty well escaped the war. But now we seem to see an abundance of free riding men, most of them footloose and somewhat adrift.

"The "A" can afford to lose the odd steer from time to time, for the feeding of a hungry man, or a traveling family. But the wholesale running off of animals, such as in the past year, will soon have all Pa's work run into the dust.

"The worst of it is, I have no idea who I can trust."

This short speech was followed by a troubled look at the two visitors.

"I need to trust someone...

"Can I trust you two?"

CHAPTER THIRTY-FOUR

The three men sat at the table; strong, rope-burned hands wrapped around their coffee mugs, a multitude of questions sorting themselves out in their minds. Somehow, they all recognized that this was the moment to be still, to think, to ponder, and, only then, to answer.

Zac was wondering how to convince this troubled rancher that the answer to his very pointed question was, 'yes, we're on your side'.

But then he immediately wondered if this was about more than lost cattle. Was there something else troubling the owner of the A-Bar? The mission Zac was on, the task he had appointed himself, was to find the men behind the theft of WO cattle, and the murder of the two cowboys. He had only ridden to the A on the off chance that the problems on the two ranches were, in fact, the same, or at least connected, in spite of the long miles between them. One single problem, you might say.

Then there was the JJ Connected. So far he had not heard mention of that situation. Were there three ranches facing the same gang of thieves? Or were there more ranches? And what about the Lazee? And Gibbs? How did it all fit together? Or did it fit at all?

He remembered situations enough from his time in battle, where the circumstances that seemed to confront the troops concealed a hoax. Where the real situation was well hidden; a surprise to be sprung at the opportune time.

Learning that your enemy was as smart as you yourself, and often smarter, was a lesson that came far too late for many decision makers in that disastrous war. The diminishing troop strength was testimony enough for that.

Central New Mexico was a huge, sparsely settled territory, with little communication between far flung ranches. It seemed unlikely that anyone was organized enough to control a rustling ring over such a vast distance. And yet, the missing cattle were strong evidence of that very thing.

Trig leaned back in his chair, lifting his coffee mug as he moved, never taking his eyes off the owner of the A-Bar. Trig, always smiling and with an almost nonchalant, joking air about him, was, in fact, a far more serious man than a casual observer might guess. On the long ride west with Claire Maddison there had been a couple of incidents where he had been misjudged.

On one occasion, a foolish young corporal from the military escort, sure somehow of a welcome, approached Claire's wagon after all the fires had died down and the camp had quieted for the night. He knew Trig was there to escort the beautiful Claire on her trip west. But he made the mistake of lightly brushing the young man away in his mind, as if he was of no importance.

The corporal was not more than three or four steps from the wagon when a quiet voice greeted him out of the dark.

"You got you just the two choices, fella. You can turn around and slink away with no one knowing about your cowardly act, or you can spend the evening bleed'n to death and moan'n out for your mama, with my blade between your ribs. Don't wish to awake the camp, so either way, we'd best do this quietly. What'll it be? Think you're man enough to die like a ghost?"

The corporal, unable to pinpoint the location of the voice, and knowing a scuffle would land him in trouble with his military superiors, made the right decision. As he turned and walked away, Claire's voice, from the rear of the sleeping wagon was barely above a whisper.

"Thank you, Trig. I had my carbine on him, but that would have woken the camp and caused all kinds of other problems."

"Goodnight, Ma'am. Sleep well."

Studying the owner of the A, and thinking back to the WO, Trig thought, Pa always advised that gitt'n two squirrels with the one hucked stone was sure to ease up on the throw'n arm.

He glanced at Zac and received a slight nod in return. Taking that as approval to express himself, Trig quietly said, "Solv'n the one situation might turn out to be solv'n two. Or mayhep, three."

Zac turned his eyes back to Lucas Wishart.

"Seems to me Mister Wishart, that you decided an answer to your question before you sent your foreman out to do what he should have already been doing. So, we've gone this far, I'd like for you to tell us the whole story. Including what you know about the JJ Connected, as well as the Lazee and Gibbs, who we've only heard of third hand, you might say."

No more was said about trust.

CHAPTER THIRTY-FIVE

After a night in the A-Bar bunkhouse followed by breakfast served up by the cook, who was still nursing a grudge about having his routine upset the afternoon before, Zac and Trig rode slowly towards the red mesa. Neither had much to say. The happenings in the vast semi-desert surrounding the A and the JJ Connected, sounded almost too strange to be true.

Zac and Trig had listened carefully as Lucas Wishart laid it all out, sitting in the cook shack the afternoon before. They had made no promises except to keep in touch and advise Lucas if anything noteworthy happened.

Zac came away satisfied that the problems involved missing cattle only, and not something deeper. Although, all put together, it still appeared to be a territory-wide matter, it was, at its base, quite simple; cattle rustling on a grand scale.

It had occurred to both Zac and Trig that when Lucas talked of trust he might be talking about his own crew. What if the men he sent to search for lost stock didn't want to find them?

As they were leaving the A, Zac shook Lucas' hand, speaking loud enough for the foreman to hear what was said.

"We'll saunter back to Albuquerque. Ask a few questions. Look around a bit. We hear or find anything; you can be sure we'll drop past with the news. We hear nothing or come to a dead end, we'll just go back to the WO and call it all a mystery.

"Thanks for the bed and the meals."

A mile out, Trig looked around to confirm that they weren't being followed, before grinning at Zac and saying, "I been try'n to figure your lead ever since you said we were rid'n back to Albuquerque. I kind of thought we'd be heading west. Out to track down the J-J ranch. Most I can guess is that you hope to throw a wasted loop at anyone curious enough to keep an eye on us, maybe especially that 'A' foreman."

Zac flashed one of his rare smiles.

"There just may be some hope for you yet."

After another slow mile Zac nodded towards the red hill and said, "A wondering kind of man with a field glass could lay atop any of these mesas and have a wide-open view for many a mile. Pretty much flat, open country all around here."

Trig took in this thought with a nod of realization.

"Never would have brought such as that to mind. Comes of being a loving, trusting sort I suppose."

He said this with a larger than usual grin.

Zac's response was to nudge his horse into a comfortable lope.

"Might just as well put out some red dust. Would make the seeing easier just in the event that someone really did climb that mesa."

Trig made no response, but the comment started him wondering if it would even be possible find a way up any of those steep cliffs.

CHAPTER THIRTY-SIX

The two riders swung off their animals and led them into the livery. Pat climbed down the ladder from the loft and greeted them with handshakes.

"I don't see no Clyde's trail'n after ya so I'm guess'n they're well and snugged down back to the "A"."

Zac said, "I suggested they be kept to the trails and out of the desert. They made no promises."

Pat responded with an unintelligible grunt.

Trig was becoming impatient with all the riding around for so little gain. There was also the truth that all the time he was away from the WO, Leonard was free to pay court to Claire, with no one there to run competition. Of course, he would never say such a thing to Zac nor anyone else.

He was hoping a bit of a push just might uncover some useful information from Pat. He hadn't forgotten how the livery man turned away from the question about the sheriff riding out to ranching country. He had been wondering about that.

After looking around the big barn to assure himself that they were alone Trig said, "Pat, thing is, about rid'n around the country, with no particular thoughts to keep a man's mind in a straight line. Apt to go off into just about any direction. Got ta remembering how you shied away from any mention of the sheriff last time we was here.

"We met Sheriff Slim Gadfry just minutes before we wandered into your stable, first time we were in town. I'd not think many would call him an overly friendly man.

"Now, if you were to be able to keep a confidence, I'd tell you just enough to tickle your ears."

With no more than a steady stare from Pat, Trig nodded and made himself comfortable by leaning back and hooking one elbow over the top rail of a horse stall. He then pushed his hat back just a bit, and grinned, before continuing.

"We. That's Zac and me, and a few others. Well, we had us a long ride. Clear up to the gold fields in Colorado. Went all that way to bring back a herd of WO animals that should have no way been up there in the first place. They weren't just wandering, Pat. They was took. A big bunch. Near the whole herd from the WO. Them that took 'em put two cowboys into their graves. Put a bullet or two into the owner too.

"Now, a man like yourself, Pat. A man that will pour his care and kindness all over a Clyde with burred feathers, why I figure that kind of man hates to hear about thefts and murder. Zac and me, well, it kind of troubles us too.

"Met some folks along the way to Colorado. They dropped some names on us. Names of a couple of ranches. Lazy A. JJ Connected. Lazee. Names of some riders too. Dawkins and Strawn. Course, they're safely tucked away in the Georgetown jail now. Fella named Gibbs was mentioned. Him bein' the foreman of the Lazee.

"Now, Pat. We. Again, that's Zac and me. We've kind of set out to see an end to the rustling and the murders. We mentioned that to your sheriff. Met with considerable unpleasantness. Kind of made me wonder.

"Then you go and clam up at a question about ol' Slim's trips out into the territory.

"Gives a man something to ponder over. It surely do."

There was silence in the barn, except for the shuffling of the horses, for a full minute.

Pat finally exhaled a long-held breath, nodded, and pointed the way to his small office and sleeping quarters.

"Let's have a seat where it's quiet, boys."

Pat pushed open the office door and took a seat in the one decent chair in the dim space. He left Zac and Trig to their own choices. Zac lifted a pile of old newspapers and penny dreadfuls off a backless, wooden chair, dropped them on the floor, and sat down. Trig went to the narrow bunk. He was surprised to see it made up, the corners tucked in military tight, a pillow neatly placed at the top.

Again, there was silence as the men studied each other.

With the silence and staring, and the nervous fidgeting having run its course, Pat cleared his throat.

"You're askin' fer a lot, boys. A lot of trust.

"I trust you and I'm wrong, I'm dead. That's not a thing to look forward to. Wouldn't take kindly to that. Not at all. Might even develop some hard feeling towards the two of you."

There was more silence as Zac and Trig waited for the livery man to continue.

Having made his decision, Pat started talking almost as if he was in the middle of the story.

"Federal Marshals. There's never enough of

'em. Spread awful thin on the ground. Don't know what they do in other parts of the country but, oh, maybe four, five months ago a fella rode into our little town. Didn't introduce himself to anyone, except by name. Tidy Walberg he called himself. Never did say just how he had found his way to Albuquerque or why he was here. Hung around near a week, jest a-sleeping in the hotel and sitt'n in the sun over there to the half-barrel chairs in front of the saloon. Just watch'n the town and visit'n with one or two folks. Most others left him alone. Didn't seem to have a thing in the world claiming his time. Everyone got used to see'n him there. Started pay'n no mind to him. I figure that's what he was aim'n for. To be there and watching, but not really seen.

"Wandered inta my barn one morn'n, like he did most morn'ns. I had been stabling his rid'n animal. Took good care of it like I always do. But he came regular, to check fer himself anyway. Surely loved that black gelding.

"Had the look of a cowboy. Dressed the part. But hard. Hard. Eyes like polished steel. Tried his best to appear friendly, jest a-sett'n out there in the sun. But folks mostly put a bit of distance between him and themselves, anyway.

"But this particular morn'n I'm talk'n about, his conversation took a different turn. Says, 'Let's you and I have a set down.'

"With no more than that he walks inta this here office and makes himself comfortable in my very own chair. I close the door and he tells me a story. Same story it seems I'm bound by duty to trust to you."

Zac and Trig looked at each other, both asking questions with their eyes. Neither wished to interrupt Pat's line of talk so the silence in the little room remained.

Pat shuffled his feet in nervousness and stood. He absently reached for the coffee pot that held a permanent place on the top of the little stove that was used for both heating and cooking. The pot hadn't been fully emptied for months. And it was never washed out. Pat had been known to threaten people with their very lives if they touched his coffee pot. He was particular about that. 'Jest nicely broke in,' he would say.

On occasion he added a half handful of ground coffee to the two inches of old grounds already settled in the bottom. He topped up the coffee dregs with water from the bucket on the shelf beside the stove, as needed.

Buying time as he thought of what to say to Zac and Trig, Pat shook the pot. Finding it in need of refilling, he lifted a dipper of water and added it to the mix. He then opened the stove door and carefully placed a couple of sticks of dried wood on the smouldering remnants of his breakfast fire.

Watching all of that, Trig was hoping the story would be told before the coffee was ready and offered around.

Re-taking his seat, Pat started the story again.

"As I'm sure you've already guessed, Tidy Walberg is a Federal Deputy Marshal. He don't advertise that around. He either made me an offer, or asked for my help, whichever way you choose to look at that.

"Now, you'll understand, I don't make no more in this business than what it takes to keep body and soul together.

"So sett'n here, and say'n noth'n at all, Tidy, reaches inta his cowhide vest pocket and lays a small leather pouch onta the tabletop. I can't see what's in it due to the tied-up laces on the top. But I hear the clunk of metal as he lays 'er down.

"He takes so long untying the leather thongs that I near jumped up and did it for him. Finally, he spreads the top open and dumps four gold double eagles out. That's more money than I'm likely to see in three, four months. Maybe longer. I'm guessing the look on my face about that time told ol' Tidy that he had me. Com'n 'n' goin', he had me. That there was a lot of money, boys.

"Jump'n to the end of the story fer ya, Tidy explained what he was about. And that he needed help. Said those double eagles were mine just fer keep'n my eyes open and sendin' a wire er two. Laid out a secret code fer me to use. Someth'n to confuse anyone down the line read'n those wires, except those that had the code on the other end. I got that there code wrote down and put away safe.

"Turns out the Federals have a few of their own agents work'n the wires, watch'n all the messages com'n and goin'. Sneaky beggars, them Federals. Never woulda guessed it.

"Turns out, too, there's another Federal out ridin' the territory right this very minute. Look'n for signs of rustl'n. Try'n to figure things out. The Federals, they been aware of the troubles for months.

"Major Gantry, him that owns the ranches they call the Lazee, three ranches all told, spread from down past the JJ Connected, all the way to the pine forests of Arizona, a far distance from here. Well, it turns out the Major, he has considerable connections in the East. Government, military and such.

"Seems a big bunch of the Major's animals came up missin'. And understandin' that a rancher can't simply hang rustlers anymore, well, he hollered for help. As Marshal Walberg tells the tale, one government man talked to another, and so on down the line. That roused the Marshals to action.

"But now, that federal that's out rid'n the trails, he ain't been heard of in some time. That's commencin' to become worrisome.

"End of this little tale, boys; you go about your search'n. Jest be real careful of what you're doin'. Don't you be light'n no fires you can't put out. Drop in here from time to time if you've got news. And keep an eye out fer a Federal named Bud Skaggett. He may be in need of help.

"And don't you be dropp'n my name inta any of yer conversations. This here livin' in a livery barn and pull'n burrs from the feathers in another man's horse may not look like much to some. But it's life anyway. And I'm kind of fond of that."

Pat's story appeared to be over but Trig still wasn't satisfied.

"Pat. I asked you about your sheriff. Slim Gadfry's actions still, somehow stick in my mind as worrisome."

Pat answered, "Best to leave him out of yer think'n. Comes to the sheriff, my advice would be ta keep yer mouth closed and yer eyes open."

With that, the livery man stood and opened the door to the office, motioning that Zac and Trig should let him get on with his work.

The coffee appeared to have been forgotten.

CHAPTER THIRTY-SEVEN

Zac and Trig talked quietly in the small café, across the road from Pat's livery. The place was noisy with the clanking of cutlery and the voices of those who had gathered for lunch.

Trig leaned a bit closer to Zac and quietly asked, "What's our plan now, boss?"

"You still feeling like seeing this thing to the end?"

"Beats stretch'n wire and fixin' fences, as I think I mentioned to someone a short while ago."

Zac laid down his knife and fork and leaned his elbows on the table, nudging his plate out of the way.

"We'll gather some supplies after lunch and head back to Santa Fe. As least we'll go a few miles towards Santa Fe before swinging west into the rough country. I keep thinking about those mesas and their flat tops. That, and the possibility of having a good look-see over the country if we were to have a glass of some kind. There's mesas all across this land. Either mesas or mountains. Must be some that a man could climb. Could sure use a glass. We had some good ones in the cavalry. I wish I had kept one."

Trig nodded his agreement and went back to his

meal. Zac pulled his plate closer and picked up his fork.

While Zac was placing an order for trail supplies at the general store, Trig walked the one block distance to a rough looking trading post. From the sidewalk in front of the small business, to every square inch of space inside, there were items on display. The counters were stacked high. Every inch of wall space was covered, and many items hung on hooks or cords from the ceiling. Some were new, many were used.

Entering the place, he walked past the saddles and leather gear without paying any particular attention. He looked over the tables of ranch clothing and grimaced as he stopped to stare at two wooden barrels overflowing with long handled tools; shovels, post hole diggers, scythe handles, picks, axes. 'Blister raisers', he thought, as he moved on.

Approaching the sales counter, where a desperately thin man stood, looking as if he could blow away in a stiff breeze, Trig spotted three sets of glasses hung by their neck straps, from nails driven into the back wall. He pointed at the items of interest and said, "Like to take a look at those glasses. They any good?"

The proprietor remained silent as he lifted down each item. Trig picked up the first one and turned to look around the small shop.

"Take it to the door. They're made for distance." The man's voice sounded as frail as he, himself looked.

Trig spent a full half hour carefully scanning the distance, first through one glass and then the others, after figuring out the adjustment knobs. Never having seen such a thing before, he was truly impressed. He decided that both he and Zac should have a pair. Setting the poorest unit aside he pushed it back across the counter, while pulling the two chosen sets towards himself.

"These seem to be the best of the three. You got any others? Better, perhaps?"

The scarecrow man seemed to pause for a moment before bending his fragile body until he could peer under the counter. Finally, he reached in and lifted out two larger and finer field glasses; brass, with blackened bodies, made with obvious craftsmanship. Had a military look to them. Showing some reluctance, he laid them on the counter. Clearly, he had hoped to sell the poorer ones first.

It took only moments for Trig to carry them to the door, one hung over his shoulder by the leather strap while he held the other in his hand. After pointing them down the street towards the distant mountains he carried them back to the sales counter.

"You been holding out on me, old man."

His smile tempered the harsh words.

"Before you go to figuring the cost on these two, you need to know that I only got so much to spend."

The two men stared at each other for a short while, as if they were in a contest of wills, before the man said, "Ten dollars. You take the two I'll settle for eighteen."

"You'll settle for fifteen, too, won't you?"

"Show me your money."

Trig lifted a leather folder from his shirt pocket and spread it open so that only he could see what was inside the sewn-in pocket. He fished through some scraps of note paper and some smaller bills before finally lifting out a ten-dollar bill. It was issued by some Philadelphia bank but no one much cared where they came from.

He was another short while finding a five to go with it but when he pulled one out and laid it on the counter with the ten, the proprietor scooped them up. They disappeared into the man's pocket so fast it was as if they had never been there.

Trig slung the glasses over his shoulder and left the store, satisfied with the efforts of the past hour.

By evening, Zac and Trig were settled into a sheltering hollow in some cottonwoods, beside the slowly meandering Rio Grande River, miles up the road towards Santa Fe. With a dinner of eggs and fresh sausage purchased in Santa Fe just hours before, the men were soon settled in for a night's sleep.

CHAPTER THIRTY-EIGHT

After their morning fire was carefully extinguished with a pan of river water, they packed up and were ready to ride. Zac had picked up two additional canteens, knowing they would be traveling in dry country. He filled them with river water and hung one each from their saddle horns.

The two stolen-cattle searchers mounted up, heading west, into the unfamiliar hills.

Looking at the great expanse of country before them, Trig said, "I'm wishing now that I had asked that trading post fella for a map. He seemed to have just about anything else a body could find a use for."

Zac nodded his agreement before saying, "You're forever telling how your father taught you tracking. Didn't he teach you directions at the same time? I'm thinking the A-Bar is south-west from here and I'm supposing the JJ Connected is out that way too. Only we're maybe ten, fifteen miles to the north. Maybe even a bit further. And still a fair way to the east."

"Well, I guess he taught me my directions alright. Can't rightly remember. I was pretty young at the time. But then, I seem to have known directions from such an early age, could be I came into this world already knowing."

Zac glanced at his riding partner. He figured Trig's grins would ease him through a good many of life's challenges.

A half day of riding put them into the hills to the west, after traveling through the sparse vegetation of the flat lands. Of course, nothing was truly flat. There were rises and hollows all along the way. But the two men figured there was nowhere rough enough to hide large bunches of cattle, east of the hills.

They saw scatterings of cattle here and there as they rode. The few animals they came close enough to see clearly, either carried unknown brands or no brand at all. There were no A-Bar or JJ Connected.

The hill country itself was dry and bleak looking, leaving Zac with fond recollections of the lovely green country he had fought through in that dreadful war, years before.

Holding to a generally westerly course, they searched out trails of previous travelers, or cattle, both of which would most likely lead to an easy way through the hills. They had no desire to explore mountain or mesa tops until they got to land closer to the A-Bar grazing grounds.

Riding through a hill enclosed valley on the third day of their explorations, they happened on a gathered bunch of both A-Bar and J-J cattle. No herders were in sight.

The two men stopped to consider the situation. Zac spoke first.

"Seems to me these animals are a long ways to the east from where Lucas Wishart said the A's grazing land was."

Trig thought for a bit before adding, "And even

further from the J-J."

Riding slowly through the herd, flipping fingers up as he rode, Trig did a rough field count. When the number became too big for accurate memory, he stopped, dismounted, and gathered up a pocket full of small pebbles. Allowing each pebble to represent one hundred animals he continued counting, moving pebbles from one vest pocket to another. He made no attempt to separate the count between the two ranches.

Riding over a small rise that separated two long, grassy valleys, Trig said, "If that gather back there is any indication, there's a lot of cattle up this way."

Repeating what Zac had said, he observed, "It seems a far distance from the ranch headquarters. On the flat land of West Texas, it wouldn't be far at all. But up here? With this land all cut to pieces with knobby hills, mesas and gullies?

"How do you suppose those animals even found this graze? And the water?"

It was Zac's turn to be silent.

After finding a similar situation in a second rocky gorge, Zac waited until they had ridden clear of the area and into the scrub land on the other side. He then turned to the south, riding directly towards a small flat-topped mesa.

"I'd sure like to find a way up that red hill."

Trig understood immediately.

"How would it be if you ride around to the west. I'll go to the east, see what we can see."

Turning to Zac with a grin he added, "As long as I'm getting those directions right, without I have Pa here to advise, I mean."

Zac grinned back and turned his gelding to the west.

It was, perhaps, four miles around the small mesa. Trig had ridden about three quarters of the distance when he spotted Zac's horse tied to a desert shrub. There was no sign of Zac. He dismounted and tied his own animal before calling out.

Zac answered the call with, "Behind that gathering of brush down there. Not much of a trail but I think we can do it. Grab those glasses and come up here. And let's try not to raise any dust."

It wasn't easy, but a half hour later the two men were crouched down on top of the red rock. The climb had included several slips and slides along the way. Zac had torn part of the knee out of his canvas pants and drawn blood from the broken skin on his knee cap.

He looked all around the rim before saying, "It's not likely anyone is watching this mesa at this particular time. On the other hand, movement would be easy to pick up."

Pointing to the south rim he said, "Let's scramble over to that jutting rock, over there on the rim. It will provide some shelter, at least.

The two men crawled on knees and elbows; their long guns cradled in the crooks of their bent arms. They had to swing the field glasses onto their backs to keep them from dragging.

Zac had to use every bit of willpower he could muster up to hide the pain in his hip.

When they eased up beside the big rock, Zac moved to the west side, and Trig crawled to the east, as if they had practiced the move.

Zac had to speak loudly to be heard over the incessant wind, but there was little fear of anyone besides Trig picking up his voice.

"Be sure you shelter that glass in the shade of the rock. A reflected sunlight flash from up here might bring all kinds of unwelcome company."

Both men were silent for several minutes while they scanned the area around the mesa.

Trig saw nothing worth mentioning but at a shout from Zac he undid some buttons on his shirt and carefully tucked the field glass inside. He then crawled around the rock and was surprised to see

Zac had moved about one hundred yards further northwest, around the rim. Trig followed him over.

When he was beside Zac, Trig said, "I hope what you've found is worth the wear and tear on my poor suffering knees. I may never be able to dance proper after this."

"Could you dance before this?"

"Not so's you'd notice, but that ain't hardly the point."

"The point, my complaining young friend, is that just off there to the west, and a bit to the north is the sweetest little trail through the hills. All shrouded in brush and a scattering of cottonwoods. But you wouldn't see the brush or trees until you were some ways down the gully. Has to be a run of water through there too. Could easily miss the whole thing from the ground. I'm thinking that's the trail we need to find and follow. Might be, oh, three miles from where our horses are tied."

The slide and scramble back down the steep slope of the mesa probably raised a visible amount of red dust, but the two climbers were unable to prevent it. In any case, the wind would make short work of it.

Carefully easing themselves out of the brush that was hiding the base of the trail, they crouched down again, taking a careful look around, seeing nothing to concern them. Almost as a single movement, they rose and stepped to their horses. They tightened their cinches and mounted.

Zac led out, heading around a rough upthrust of rock before turning towards the northwest. Trig followed, sitting loosely in the saddle as he turned first to his right and then to the left, looking for movement. After Zac lead them behind the craggy rocks, Trig relaxed a bit.

They had to backtrack twice to escape dead

end trails, but finally Zac was convinced the small opening before them was the one they were seeking. Again, Trig took a careful look around before entering the opening.

The clatter of iron shod hooves on jagged rock was soon replaced with near silence, as the animals stepped on centuries of accumulated dead leaves and pine needles. Almost immediately they were riding among cattle, mostly A-Bar, but now, for the first time, seeing some Lazy E, or Lazee as the riders called it. The first bunch was gathered around a small trickle of water. The grass was grazed short. It was clear to both Trig and Zac that the herd had been there for some time.

Trig began counting again but finally gave it up when he saw small bunches gathered in several side canyons. He pushed his horse up beside Zac.

"Without even an accurate count we can figure that losses of this size would cripple most ranches. I'm thinking those men Lucas Wishart sent out from the A to search the hills for cattle, had to be a part of the problem. No one could miss finding all this. That casts a lot of suspicion onto Bobby Cromwell."

Zac, with his eyes firmly fixed into the distance ahead of them simply nodded, and then motioned to be quiet. Trig caught on, following Zac's gaze into the treed hillside about a quarter mile ahead. There, dimly seen through the green growth was just the slightest hint of wood smoke.

The fire that had to be the source of the curling smoke was undoubtedly small, held that way intentionally, to disguise the camper's presence. The smoke lost itself in the pine trees that crowded the area, again, with the aid of the breeze.

Knowing that the movement of their horses, even with their steps being quieted by the debris on the ground, was sure to be picked up by any careful camper, they dismounted. They proceeded at a wary walk, leading their horses. They stopped when Trig spotted a dim foot trail angling up the slope. Tying their animals, and carrying their carbines with them, they made their slow, silent way from tree to tree. They soon stepped onto a flat area one hundred yards east of the source of the smoke.

Dropping to his knees while he studied the way ahead, Zac motioned for Trig to get down. Trig sank into a crouch and moved in front of Zac. With no words, he indicated that Zac should stay where he was while he made his way forward.

As Zac watched his riding partner easing his way through the low-lying shrubbery and under the pines, he thought, 'He's good. I could never move that silently.'

It was only a matter of half a minute before Trig spoke.

"Stand fast, friend."

The man at the fire stiffened and turned his head to see who was speaking.

Trig nodded at the camper and said, "Don't you go to gett'n riled up. Anyway, I've got the clear drop on you. Would I be right in figur'n that you might be Bud Skaggett? There's folks worrying about you Mister Skaggett. Think'n you might be in some kind of trouble after not hearing from you in some time."

Zac rose and walked forward as Bud Skaggett said, "I am in some difficulty, you might say. I'm plumb out of coffee. If you could spare me a bit of that elixir, I would welcome you to my humble abode."

Trig rose to his feet and entered the snug camp.

"Trig Mason here, Mister Skaggett. And this is my friend, Zac Trimbell. Fella named Pat sends his greetings."

"Well, I know a Pat or two. Here and there. We'll say no more about that for the time being. So, now I know your names, or at least the names you're using. But that doesn't tell me who you are or why you're here."

Zac said, "All in good time sir. But for now, I'd like to get our horses hidden away. If you could tell me where I could do that, I'd appreciate it."

Accepting the situation, Bud Skaggett rose to his feet and stepped towards Zac.

"Follow me."

Trig was left alone in the camp while the horses were moved. Without touching anything, he gave the layout a thorough examination. He saw nothing at all that would confirm the identity of the camper. Of course, that might change if he were to look through the saddle bags leaning against the bole of a big pine. But that would be a serious infringement of accepted camp etiquette.

Less than ten minutes later Zac and Bud re-entered the camp. The horses were staked out in a little swale a hundred yards away.

Bud accepted the small sack of coffee from Zac as if it were gold, free for the taking.

"Purely do miss my coffee."

Trig thought of Pat, who used the same grounds over and over. He thought it best to say nothing.

Bud refilled his blue enameled coffee pot from the little trickle that wound its way down the slope behind the camp. Placing it on the fire that Trig had rebuilt, he sat back down beside his saddle bags, his back to the pine tree.

"Now. Tell me who you are and exactly why you're here."

Zac smiled at the man before saying, "This will take a few minutes."

"That don't matter. I've got nothing but time now that there's coffee in the pot."

Alternating between Zac and Trig, the story was told, leaving out Pat's full identity.

CHAPTER THIRTY-NINE

After Zac completed his telling, he looked at Bud Skaggett.

"Now, perhaps you can tie our findings together with yours and we can wrap this thing up. Kind of like to get home sometime soon."

After a brief pause the marshal said, "I've found cattle. A lot of cattle. In those two valleys you mentioned coming through today, and a couple of others. All of them well off the normal grazing range of the A or the J-J. Most carry one of the three brands you've mentioned. but some are unbranded. Just a few others showing marks I know nothing about.

"Lots of hidden canyons up here, like the ones you rode through. My guess is that they'll all be ranched in the next few years. The ones that hold grass and water, anyway. But right now, the riders are still searching them out. Big country. Take some time. I expect the Indians and Mex's have known all this area for decades, or longer. But the ranchers have still got a lot to learn about the country.

"I've pretty much seen all the riders that appear to be involved in this steal. But I have no way of knowing their names. All I can go by is the brands on their horses. They're all A-Bar except for one J-J Connected. Haven't seen any Lazee riders."

The three men sat silently, thinking through the situation. Trig finally spoke up.

"There's no way we, just the three of us, can handle this job. The local law is no help at all, and the marshals don't have the manpower. If we can grab a couple of riders and take them to the A, I'm thinking one or two might sing us a song, identify the other riders and the ringleaders, just to save their own miserable hides.

"That should be enough to bring in the marshals with some force.

"Then it will be up to the ranchers to get their animals dug out of these hills."

Bud nodded as Trig was speaking.

"First light tomorrow morning we'll take their camp. I was planning on it anyway, but having you here makes success a little more likely."

Knowing it would be a challenge to roust out determined rustlers, both Zac and Trig remained quiet, thinking on the possibilities. And the risks.

Riding easy in the saddle just before first light the following morning, Zac and Trig tracked the young marshal through the rocks and trees of the enclosed canyon. Bud had said the rustler's camp was near to a full mile to the west, right at the entrance to the hidden graze. Before mounting they had checked and secured everything on their saddles and packs that could move or clatter or make a noise. They then rode forward as silently as possible.

The sky was barely breaking into a dull gray when Bud dropped his hand as a signal that they were nearing the thieves' camp. Each man carried his carbine at the ready, Bud and Trig, across their laps, Zac, with his Henry hanging beside his right leg, as was his long habit.

They pulled to a stop, with Bud pointing into the shelter of some broken boulders that had tumbled down the small mountain years before. Behind and beside the boulders they saw a solid growth of small pines.

But as careful as they had been, something had tipped off the other camp. Probably just some little thing, a click of a hoof on a stone, a huff of exhaled breath from a horse, a squeak of saddle leather. Not much. But enough.

Before the three riders had time to agree on their approach, the dawn exploded with gunfire. Without warning, at least four gunmen started pouring lead out of the shelter of the greenery. It was the darkness that prevented the deaths of Zac and his partners.

But it didn't prevent a bullet from slamming into Trig's hide, just above his beltline, close to his left side, grazing the top of his hip bone. He was startled by the sudden pain, but he held onto his weapon and his ride in spite of being jostled and tossed about in the saddle. His gelding plunged in terror, nearly throwing him to the ground. A firm hand on the reins and a gentle word calmed the animal.

Ignoring the pain as best he could, Trig eased off his horse, turned it loose with a slap of his hat and limped back towards the rustler camp. He could feel blood running down his pant leg but he could do nothing about it. Leaning on a large, zagged rock, he lifted his weapon and peered around the edge, hoping to see something to shoot at. There was nothing specific, but there was a suggestion of movement shadowed against the darker outlines of the pines.

He emptied his carbine into the greenery, although he could see only an unclear outline of men, and, here and there, a flash of gunfire.

Squeezing the trigger without knowing exactly what he was shooting at went against everything he had ever been taught or believed. But their lives were at stake. He would do what had to be done.

A scream of agony was heard. Since there were many guns speaking, it was impossible for Trig to know if it was his shot that had struck home.

Bud was on the ground, gasping in pain from a shot through his thigh. He, too, had held on to his carbine, although his horse had run off, bucking and squealing in fear. Knowing he had to fight or die, the federal marshal rolled onto his stomach and poured all the lead the carbine held into the shooters' hideaway.

Seeing Bud lying in the open, trying to reload, and with the morning beginning to lighten up, Trig pushed his own pain out of his mind while he made a mad, lopsided dash to where the wounded man lay.

"Hang on to that weapon, Bud."

Trig grabbed the back of Bud's shirt collar. Fuelled by fear and adrenaline, Trig ran, tugging the injured man across the rocky ground. Bud screamed in pain at the rough treatment, but he was soon amongst the shelter of some small rocks.

The two men collapsed into a bleeding, pain-filled heap. They immediately straightened themselves out as best they could and reached into their pockets for ammunition.

Zac was left alone with the others temporarily out of the fight. In the semi darkness no one could see where or what they were shooting at. That type of battle had never appealed to the ex-cavalry man.

The firing from the rustlers had died down. Whether from lack of ammunition or because of death or injury, Zac had no way to know. What he did know was that he was a well experienced warrior, sitting on a steady animal that had heard firing and smelled powder smoke many times. And having held his Henry in reserve while Trig and Bud were shooting, he had a weapon holding fifteen .44 cal. shells at the ready.

During his time with the cavalry it had been drummed into every man that to be caught with everyone having an empty weapon was an invitation to death. Zac learned the lesson well.

The silence from the rustler camp suggested that they had not learned the lesson, all emptying their weapons at the same time.

It was time to attack. To ride among the enemy. To put a final stop to the action.

The sun had lightened the morning enough to see, although dimly.

Zac had jumped his horse just three strides to the side when the shooting started. Although it always felt like a lot of time was passing when the weapons opened up, in reality it was only seconds. But now it was his turn.

He eased the animal back towards the enemy and let the old cavalry mount feel the spurs, something that rarely happened. The well experienced gelding moved from a standing start into a full charge in three strides. With the Henry held in one hand and with his head sheltered as close to the animal's neck as humanly possible, Zac rode into battle. His horse ducked under a low hanging pine branch and charged around the boulders.

One man rose up, his handgun at the ready. Zac shot him through the body. The shooter crumpled to the ground as the big gelding rode over him, slamming his broken body against the trunk of a large pine. Two other men were down and not moving. The fourth rustler, hunkered behind a large rock, threw his gun down in defeat and raised his hands.

"Stop. Don't shoot. We're done."

Zac twisted the horse in a circle, trying to take in everything around the camp. Seeing no more threat, he said, "Any more of you in the bush? Don't you be lying to me."

"No more. And that's the truth. Just me now. You got these others."

Zac held not one ounce of pity for the terrified man. It might have been easier to just shoot him right off, but they needed a living witness to the rustling.

Zac motioned with his Henry towards where Trig and Bud lay wounded.

"Shuck your gun belt and walk out there. I got two men that need care. You can help by bringing a pot of clean water. You make a move to do anything I don't like this will be your last sunrise."

As the thief was struggling to his feet and making his way around the boulders, Zac swung to the ground and went to the other three. A quick check confirmed that two were already dead. The third, the one Zac had shot, was still alive, but the way his crumpled body was bleeding, it was obvious he didn't have long.

Zac quickly gathered up all the weapons he could see and toted them out of the small camp.

An hour later, with the dead men tied across their saddles and with Trig and Bud treated to the best of Zac's ability, with the meager provisions on hand, the group headed out, needing to reach the A-Bar in one long ride.

Monty Abbot, the captured A-Bar rustler, led out at a steady walk, driving the three loaded horses before him. Trig and Bud followed closely, each suffering with their wounds, but sitting their saddles as best they could.

As Monty was mounting up, Trig said, "You got to remember fella, this bullet through my side came nowhere near my trigger finger. And it left me in no good mood for nonsense. Ain't never been shot before. Don't know as it's an experience I care to repeat. And just so's you'll understand, I'll advise you that it hurts like you've been losing a battle with a whole swarm of red ants. You want to avoid that if possible. Way to do that is to give me no trouble or the pleasure of shooting you."

Monty said nothing but he was careful in his actions.

Zac wondered if the A-Bar rider was struggling with guilt after telling the story of the rustling, and his part in it. He also gave detailed information on the activities of others.

While the confessions may save him from the hangman's rope, Zac was sure the man would question and re-question it all, as time went by. It's a hard thing to turn on your friends to save your own hide. Monty would have that to live with.

Zac brought up the rear of the cavalcade, a full half hour later.

He had let the others take the lead. He needed a bit of space between them to hide his struggle from their eyes.

Although always unpredictable, his emotions and depression had been pretty well under control since leaving the gold camp in Colorado, and the meetings with his old friends. Those meetings were like taking on new life for him. Like manna for his soul. Even if only for a short while.

The ride back to the WO had been almost pleasant in the late spring sun. In spite of the never-ending, underlying sadness and, sometimes the sense of pointlessness left over from his losing war, he was hoping the good feelings would last. And they did. On the surface at least. Right until the guns started howling out their deadly message, just a few minutes before.

But even with him sitting out the initial few

seconds of battle, holding himself in reserve, the thunder of six carbines all firing at the same time, the screams of wounded and dying men and terrified horses, the stinging smell of burnt powder, the blood, the death, all brought back dreadful, unbidden memories of war. Memories he had never been fully successful at pushing down. Memories that never failed to drive him, emotionally, to his knees.

The first year following the war, these episodes came frequently and seriously, without warning. Lately he had been feeling better, although he was not nearly the stable contented man he was, years ago, on his little farm with his wife and young daughter to work and care for.

He tried to be cautious of the situations he got himself into. But somehow, trouble seemed to follow him. Or even, sometimes, get there first and he would find it waiting for him.

Standing beside his saddled gelding, ready to ride, he wrapped his arms around the cantle and the pommel, and laid his forehead against the leather seat, gritting his teeth. He took several deep breaths. He felt shudders warp their way through his very being. It was all beyond his immediate control.

A blackness so dark that he couldn't have described it, overtook him momentarily. As so often happened when the blackness came, something warned him not to move, not even to shuffle his feet, lest he fall into the black hole beneath, and be swallowed up.

There came an unexplainable sadness, deep and gripping, accompanying the blackness of soul.

He was silent, but inside, his heart was weeping. Faster than could be told, images of battle flashed through his mind. And names. Names of men dead these many years. Men he had fought beside. Men he had been friends with. Men he had cared for. All gone. In the insanity of combat, they were all taken away.

Images of his dead wife and little girl followed immediately. He saw these even as his mind flipped over to the scene of their burning cabin. He knew he had cried out at these sights, but that seemed also to be beyond his control.

As had happened so often in the past, he wanted to quit, to lay down in the grass and close his eyes. To give in to the blackness, if that would somehow bring him peace.

But his rational mind told him he couldn't stay there. He couldn't give in. There was a task to finish. Men were depending on him. Wounded men. A part of him didn't care, but a better part rose to the occasion.

Gripping the horn tight enough to crush the leather, he lifted his foot into the stirrup. Sitting astride, he nudged the animal into motion.

His eyes hurt. There was a striking pain running through his forehead. The temptation to turn around and just ride away was almost overwhelming.

But duty is an ingrained, learned and accepted part of a good man's life. So, he followed after the other riders, the reins draped across the animal's neck, while he held the horn with both hands, his eyes closed tightly, moisture working its way out of their corners and dribbling down his cheeks.

He wished he could remember how to pray. Really pray.

After a slow mile of blind riding, knowing his gelding would follow the other horses, he pushed himself upright. He lifted the canteen and took a quick taste of the tepid water. He swallowed several times in an attempt to rid himself of the salty bile clogging his throat. He shook his head. He wiggled his shoulders back and forth. He turned and studied their back trail.

It was going to be a long day. He hoped for no additional trouble along the way.

A slow fifteen-mile ride led them to the northern edge of the A-Bar range. It wasn't long until they saw bunches of cattle and two riders, off in the distance.

Zac rode to the side, pointed the Henry into the air, and fired off one shot. When the riders turned his way, he stood in the stirrups, lifted his hat and waved it as a signal. Zac could see the two men talking, but they were far out of reach for sound.

After a short wait the riders pointed their animals towards Zac's group.

With the help and guidance of the two new cowboys, they were soon riding into the ranch yard. They had both taken a troubling look at Monty Abbot but asked no questions.

The arrival of the cavalcade seemed to bring everyone at the ranch into the yard. The two women, again, one young and one older, stayed on the porch.

Before the riders even had a chance to dismount, Lucas Wishart wordlessly went from horse to horse, gripping each dead man's hair and turning the face outwards, trying for recognition. Seeing two A-Bar men among the three, his face paled and his lips trembled, seemingly lost for words. With his eyes showing his agony, he looked at the mounted men.

So quietly he could hardly be heard he said, "Monty?"

The ashamed cowboy couldn't look at this good man he had double crossed and stolen from. He simply stared at the ground with his shoulders hunched as if he was waiting for a blow to his back.

When Lucas turned his eyes back to Zac, he was surprised to see that man holding his Henry on Bobby Cromwell. A glance around showed him that Trig had also drawn down on the foreman, even though it was all the young man could do to stay in the saddle.

The federal marshal was stretched out forward, his arms wrapped around the horse's neck,

Into the silence Zac spoke with a voice as hard as granite.

"Bobby Cromwell, you unbuckle your belt and let 'er drop. Any other movement will find you in your grave this night."

Lucas spoke up in shock.

"What's this all about?"

Without taking his eyes from the foreman, Zac answered, "Why, sir, it's about rustling, murder and lying. It's about your foreman here, him and the Albuquerque sheriff, being the leaders of the pack of scoundrels that have caused so much trouble the past year or two.

"That's why your crew could never find the cattle. They didn't want you to find them."

Lucas turned towards his foreman.

"Bobby? Surely not!"

For a moment Zac was fearful the foreman was going to lift his handgun. Take a chance against two aimed carbines. But silently one of the other cowboys had stepped up to the foreman's side. With a deft move he slicked the Colt out of its holster, leaving Bobby Cromwell unarmed.

Lucas took the three steps needed to close on his foreman. Without a word he smashed his fist into the man's face, breaking his nose and sending him to the ground in a shower of blood.

CHAPTER FORTY

With the ranch yard turned into a jumble of excited voices, a cowboy snuck around the corner of the cookhouse, where he had tied his working horse, seeking his escape. To get out of the yard it was necessary that the man drive his running horse right past the gathered men.

With a shout of alarm, the wrangler, forever carrying a coiled lariat in his hand, took several running steps as he unwound the rope. With three twirls and a long throw, the rope fell over the escaping man's head, coming to a stop around his chest, as the wrangler dug his heels into the yard's red dirt. The cowboy flew backwards out of the saddle, hitting the ground hard and lying there without moving. He was soon trussed up and standing before Lucas.

Lucas looked like he just might cry in frustration. Zac, studying the ranch owner, thought it more likely that Lucas would lift his own Colt and bring instant justice right there in the A-Bar ranch yard.

It was what many ranchers would have done.

Zac stepped from the saddle and laid his hand on Lucas' shoulder.

"We'll let the law sort it all out. We don't know

the whole of it yet. Anyway, we have two wounded men that need care. You can do as you wish with the bodies."

Lucas allowed the tension to leak out of his shoulders.

"You're right, of course."

Talking to no one in particular, he spoke to his crew. There was a distinct heaviness in his voice.

"If there's any men here who really do ride for the A-Bar, I'd like if you would tie these men securely in the barn. He gestured towards his foreman, the escaping rider and Monty Abbot. Two of you stand guard. If they get loose, I'll have your hides."

The two Wishart women had walked down from the porch, drawn by the sight of the marshal draped over his horse's neck. The older of the two, who was obviously Mrs. Wishart, first looked in wonder at the disgraced foreman. She then turned to the marshal.

Most town women would have blanched at the sight of the blood-soaked pant leg, with fresh blood still finding its way through the rough bandage Trig had tied on the marshal, and then through the canvas pants. But this well-experienced ranch lady did no such thing. Neither did the younger girl, probably the daughter.

By carefully laying forward and swinging his un-wounded hip and leg over the saddle, and ignoring the stirrup, Trig managed to slide down onto his one good foot. The jolt as his foot touched the ground sent screaming shivers through his body.

He was still gripping the horn when something caused his horse to sidestep. Unable to stay with the horse's movements, the young man fell to the ground. A gasp of pain escaped his tightly held lips.

This caused the two women to cry out in surprise, staring at another blood-soaked man.

Lucas said, "A couple of you men help that fella off his horse and tote them into the bunk house. We'll see what can be done for them."

Mrs. Wishart overrode her husband's directions.

"You'll do no such a thing. That bunk house full of half-washed cowboys and saddle blankets is no place for wounded men. Carry them carefully to the house. Put them in the back bedroom. There's two beds in there.

"Glenda, you run up and see that all is in readiness. And start some water to heating."

Lucas hunched his shoulders in defeat.

"Do as she says men."

Two men immediately stepped up and gently worked the marshal off his horse.

Lucas then turned to Zac.

"You look like you could use some grub. And some coffee."

When the two men were seated in the cookhouse, Lucas asked, "Where exactly did you find these men?"

Before Zac could answer Lucas asked a second question.

"And what about the cattle?"

Zac told the shortened story, finishing with, "We couldn't get an accurate count, but there are a lot of cattle hidden away. The three brands are all there. A-Bar, J-J and Lazee. There's a few others too. You'll have some work getting them all home.

"Going by shirttail guess I'd say the cattle are about twenty miles north-east of the ranch. We found three canyons holding animals. There could be more. The men were camped at the entrance to the closest canyon."

Lucas listened silently. With a pained look on his

face he hunched his shoulders and rocked his head from side to side, as if to shake away the truth.

"You get some rest. I'll send a couple of men to ride to both the JJ Connected and the Lazee, in the morning. Too late today, but they need to know.

"It's a long ride to the Lazee. This thing won't be settled just yet, a while. It won't be brought to an end until the Major has his say."

After a night's sleep and a thorough wash at the basin behind the bunk house, Zac ate his breakfast and then made his way to the sick room. Both men were awake, but neither were up, nor looking like they were ready to take on a day's work.

The younger of the Wishart women, Glenda, the daughter, was gently wiping a wet rag over Monty Abbot's forehead, looking very concerned and caring.

Before Zac could ask any questions Trig spoke.

"Zac, I ain't going to enjoy it none but I need you to shoot me again. Just a little bit you understand."

"I've been tempted a time or two but exactly why would you wish that right at this time?"

Trig managed to find a grin, in spite of his pain and discomfort.

"This here no good marshal fella, he's taking up all of Glenda's time and attention. Play acting, and all. Just because they had to dig out a bullet or some such little thing, she's all full of sympathy. The scoundrel's playing it up for all he's worth. Ain't half as sick as he's making out to be. I can't get so much as a 'how are you this morning?' out of her."

His short speech was interrupted by the young lady's giggle.

"Here I lay suffering something awful and those two don't pay the slightest attention. Doubtful if they know what time of day it is. I figure…"

"Don't you be figuring a single thing, young man. You go to figuring, you'll find yourself out in the bunkhouse fending for yourself."

The voice of Mrs. Wishart left no doubt as to her meaning.

Trig responded with an even bigger grin.

"Yes, Ma'am."

Zac shook his head, turned and left, with no further questions asked nor answered.

Lucas had two trusted cowboys picked out and saddled for the ride to the J-J.

Zac walked over and said, "You hold on just a minute. I'll ride with you."

The three of them were soon on their way. Although they were instructed to continue on to the Lazee after carrying the news to the J-J, they were hoping someone at the other ranch would offer to make the ride.

By mid-morning the trio from the A were riding into the yard of the J-J Connected. Their entry was noted by a black and white dog, who ran around the corner of the barn, barking threats.

Zac could immediately see that it was a much more recently established spread, not showing the stability nor the prosperity of the A-Bar.

Jeremiah Bodkin, known as Buck, owner of the J-J, was watching them from the door of the barn. There was no one else in sight.

One of the 'A' cowboys said, "Morn'n, Buck. Got a piece of news for ya."

"Ease yourselves down. You know where the corral is. We'll go to the house for a sit-down."

The J-J had no cook house. With a small crew it was still possible for Mrs. Bodkin to feed the men, along with her young family. She was never without a pot of coffee and a slice of home-baked bread.

After he was introduced to Zac, Buck led the group into the kitchen. He repeated the introduction of Zac for his wife.

Taking his regular seat at the head of the table he asked, "So what brings you men over here this morning?"

Over coffee and fresh bread spread with sweet molasses, Zac again told the shortened version of recent events.

Both Buck and his wife paled as they listened. Mrs. Bodkin cried out and buried her face in her hands when she was told of the dead J-J rider. The men were silent, allowing her some time to recover. Finally, she looked at her husband with a drained expression.

"Not Tony. Surely not. He's such a nice young man. How could he do this to the J-J? To you? To us?"

Buck, his eyes showing the pain the news brought, offered no response.

Zac waited for someone else to come up with an answer, but nothing was said. Leaving the agonizing questions unanswered, he said, "Do you have a man that could ride to the Lazee? Lucas figures the Major needs to be in on the wrap up."

The question was interrupted by the dog's barking again. The barking was followed closely by the rattle of steel rimmed wheels on the sun-baked dirt of the yard. As Buck was rising from the table to see who their new visitors were, they all heard a quiet, but firm, "Whoa there now," as the team was brought to a halt at the hitch rail outside the fenced house yard.

Recognizing the voice, Buck stood.

"Why, that's the Major now. I'd know that voice anywhere."

Stepping to the already opened door, Buck hollered out, "Why, Major Gantry. You're always welcome, but what brings you all the way over here?"

The Major wrapped the reins around a metal hook fastened to the dashboard and stepped to the ground. For a large man, both tall and husky, his actions were swift and precise. He reached his hand out to the J-J Connected owner.

"How do, Jeremiah? It's been too long. I hope you are all well."

Then, looking past Buck he spotted Mrs. Bodkin standing on the front porch. He immediately lifted his hat, holding it in front of his chest.

"Good morning to you, Missus Bodkin. My Philomena sends her greetings. Mentioned you in particular when we started out on this long, dusty ride."

"Thank you, Major. Be sure to carry our good wishes back with you."

Buck said, "You must have camped the night. You and your men will be ready for a rest and some refreshment. Come into the house, all of you. Betty will be putting on fresh coffee. I'm sure she'll soon have some breakfast ready for you also."

Turning to the two riders that accompanied the Major, Buck said, "Gibbs, Gord, welcome. When you've cared for your animals please join us at the house."

The Major nodded at his men, giving them silent permission to join the larger group. He then chuckled a bit, rubbing his sore back.

"Thank you, Jeremiah. I do believe a walk around the yard will help to straighten out these old bones before we take up your hospitality. We'll tarry just a bit. Then we must get on to the A-Bar. But tell me, is there any news?"

"Come to the house. We'll talk."

Zac was standing halfway between the house and the newly arrived buggy. The Major had glanced at him, turned away and then swung his eyes back. He was a moment, clearly attempting to identify this familiar face. It took only the measure of a few breaths.

"Trimbell? Trooper Trimbell? Is...? Why, I believe it is!"

"Good morning, Major. When I heard the name mentioned a few weeks ago I wondered. But I never knew you as a cattleman, so I said nothing, figuring I'd find out soon enough."

The two men met halfway and shook hands. The Major half turned to his rear while still holding Zac's hand.

"You'll remember Sergeant Gibbs. Johnny, come say hello to Trooper Trimbell."

The handshakes were followed by a comment from the Major.

"We got separated there towards the end, Trooper. I heard no more about you. But that was not uncommon. Whole armies got separated from one another. I'm afraid the desire to survive superseded the wondering about others. So many were lost. Bad time. I'm beyond happy to see you standing here."

"I'm pleased to see the two of you looking well, also."

The Major asked, "How are you involved in this affair we are so troubled with, Trimbell? And before you tell me that, tell me what name you are known by now. It's best we let the old designation slide by the board."

He didn't seem to see the irony between the statement and his continuing use of the title, 'Major'.

"Thank you, Major. My given name is Isaac. But somehow, I was dubbed as Zac during the war. That name has stuck. It's all these folks know me by so it's good enough."

"Zac it is then. Come. Walk a bit with me as I stretch these old, worn joints."

They hadn't taken many steps, with Gibbs trailing a restful three paces behind, when the Major said. "So, tell me. What's going on? The home ranch of the Lazy-E is in a beautiful mountain valley surrounded on all sides by pine forests. There's miles of grass and plentiful water. We love the place, but we are very isolated. News can take weeks to arrive. Sometimes months.

"This rustling thing has been going on long enough. I discussed it with Gibbs a few days ago and we decided it was time. If the law couldn't deal with it, the Lazy-E would do it. I've men enough. And more. But first we agreed to get the facts.

"You'll remember how we were so often short on the facts during that unfortunate conflict. That shortage was the genesis of much pain and misery. So, we are here to get the facts. Anything you can tell me will help."

Less than an hour later, the group, expanded to include Buck Bodkin and another J-J rider, was on the way to the Lazy-A. There were still a few hours of the day left when the bunch from the J-J arrived.

CHAPTER FORTY-ONE

The A-Bar cook scrambled around and laid out an early dinner. As the men were eating, the Major, who now had a full understanding of the situation, asked, "So, Zac, since the wounded marshal is not likely to leave that comfortable bed, nor the ministrations of the vary caring Miss Glenda Wishart, and your man is not going to be riding for a few days, that would seem to leave you as the leader of this group. What is your plan, if you don't mind me asking?"

Zac laid down his fork and thought about the Major's question. The question was bound to come, and Zac had been considering his answer.

"Any leadership I hold is about as unofficial as it could possibly be. I would happily defer to you, Major. You or Lucas, either one, with just one thought of my own. I would hate for the Albuquerque sheriff to get wind of all that's transpired. He would most likely be gone before ever we got there if that were to happen.

"I'm in favor of setting out for town right now, at least a few of us. we need to get the man and his deputies under our control if we have any hope of finding out if there are others involved that we don't yet know about. We can sort it all out after that."

"I agree totally," answered the Major.

Lucas offered no objection.

Raising his voice, the Major said, "Men, everyone free to ride please see to your mounts and prepare yourselves. We leave in one quarter hour."

With that he stood and stretched his hand out to Lucas Wishart. "Lucas, thank you for your hospitality. Please thank your cook for us."

"And please thank Missus Wishart and Glenda for their care of the wounded men. We'll take our leave now."

Lucas stood up with a serious look on his face.

"Not without me and a couple of my riders, you won't."

He shouted to the men who were crowding towards the cookhouse door.

"Emmett, Felix. Saddle up. The rest of you men stay close to the ranch yard. Keep an eye out for trouble. And set a two-man guard over night.

"A few of you get those prisoners mounted and tied to their saddle horns. Lay those three bodies over their saddles and bring them along. I don't want them buried here on the 'A'. Let's move it."

Buck Bodkin spoke above the clamor of voices in the yard.

"Major, Lucas, as much as I would love nothing more than to ride to town, seeing an end to these troubles, I can't spare the three men I have on payroll. I can't leave the ranch and my family undefended. I'll have to ride home, leaving just the one J-J man to ride with you. I trust you to keep all our interests in mind in whatever has to be done."

Lucas shook his neighbor's hand.

"You go look after your family. We'll clean this up.

"When we're ready to go for the cattle I'll get the news to you."

The last rider had mounted and turned towards the yard gate when the sound of a slamming screen door caught their attention. The slamming of the door and a raised voice. As he slowly shuffled across the dusty yard, holding one hand over his wound, Trig called out to the mounted men.

"Y'all went and forgot to tell me you was setting out, did ya? Had to hear that news from Missus Wishart. She who's happy to see the end of this Texan, if I have the right of it.

"I'm goin' to have to shop around for a new group of friends, I can see that plain enough. Sett'n off by yourselves! Leav'n me lay'n here a-bed. I never in all my born days heard the like."

Zac lifted his hat and rubbed his fingers through his hair.

"Thought you were bound to a sick bed. All moaning and crying out for help from that pretty nurse."

Trig just waved the comment off and went for his horse. He tried to hide his soreness but wasn't really fooling anyone. Secretly, he was happy the wrangler was there to throw his saddle and gear on the gelding.

The buggy held the gathered men to a steady, but not fast trot. The normal two-hour ride into Albuquerque was lengthened to almost three hours. The evening was well advanced, with darkness threatening, before they rode down the dusty road into town. Zac lead them to Pat's livery.

Pat stood in the wide doorway studying the arriving men. His eyes fell to Zac. Wordlessly, he asked what was happening.

For fear of revealing Pat's secret, Zac simply said, "Evening, Pat. You got room for a few horses in the barn? They've got some miles on them. I'd like if they could be inside."

Pat was carefully slow in speaking to the group.

"Step down out here and walk your animals in. Take any empty stall, as suits you. You can put the buggy under the roof off to the side.

"Better walk them bodies down to Mendoza, over there on the next block, behind the saloon.

"I see men tied to their saddles. Assuming they're prisoners, you best take them over to the sheriff's lockup, just down the street. I don't want them no-where near the barn."

He hesitated, lifted his chin to give directions, sharing a knowing look with Zac.

"Sheriff Gadfry's over to the cantina having his evening dinner, far as I know."

Pat locked his eyes on Zac, who simply stepped to the ground, showing nothing by his looks.

Zac walked his gelding into the barn and stalled him. He was just reaching for the cinch strap when Pat spoke quietly.

"I'll get that fer ya. You'll be want'n to see ol' Slim if I got my guess right."

The three prisoners were being walked down the road as Zac came out of the livery. He spoke to the cowboys leading them.

"Be sure you put Monty Abbot in a cell by him-self. We don't want any harm to come to him."

He then crossed the road to the saloon, carrying his Henry as if it was an extension of his right arm.

Several men were standing outside the small adobe, the crowd at the livery having caught their attention. The sheriff wasn't among them.

Zac entered the dim establishment, paused for a moment to get his bearings and to allow his eyes to adjust, and then walked to Slim Gadfry's table. The sheriff tried to ignore him.

"Got some prisoners for you, Sheriff. You need to come and see to their confinement."

"I told you plain. I got no use for vigilantes. And

I've got no interest in your prisoners."

Without warning, Zac swung the Henry. The smack on the side of the sheriff's head was a sickening sound. Slim Gadfry slid silently from his chair and lay, out cold, in the filthy sawdust of the cantina floor.

Zac bent and lifted the sheriff's Colt. He then quickly ran his hand over the man's clothing to check for other weapons. He found a large Bowie knife thrust into a sheaf at the back of his belt, but nothing else.

Zac looked around the room before calling out, "I need a couple of you men to tote ol' Slim over to his office."

No one spoke or moved.

Zac hunched his shoulders in resignation and caught the back of the sheriff's collar. He dragged him unceremoniously across the floor, leaving a wide tracing in the sawdust. He kneed the door open and yanked the heavy burden across the boardwalk, then bounced him down the three steps leading to the road.

At that time, a couple of the men who had ridden to town from the A-Bar saw what he was doing and came to take over the task.

With the prisoners locked up and everything settled down for the night, the cowboys had a single drink after their dinners and retired to the livery. They would play some matchstick poker over a couple of hay bales for an hour or so and then move to the loft for the night.

Trig had taken a hotel room, feeling that his barely healing bullet wound needed something better than a bed of hay. Earlier he had visited the doctor. That man simply looked at the wound, grunted an unintelligible comment, cleaned it up with some foul-smelling liquid, wrapped it in a clean cloth and asked for two dollars.

Zac joined the Major and Johnny Gibbs at their table in the dining room. Lucas Wishart walked in a few minutes later. Over drinks, they discussed just enough of the war to put it behind them, thankful to have survived. Zac told them nothing at all about losing his family or the struggles he constantly faced with his mind and memories. He had become more private as the years passed.

Wishing he could avoid the topic but knowing he owed it to Johnny Gibbs, he told how the rustlers were using his name as a cover and how a couple of them had implied that the Lazee and the Major himself, were the gang leaders.

After a period of silence, the Major promised, "Not to worry. We'll put an end to that tale if it's repeated down here."

Remembering what a fierce fighter and patriot Johnny Gibbs had been, Zac was surprised at how silent and submissive the man was with the Major. He wondered if the old sergeant was suffering some of the same things as was himself. But he decided it was a good subject to avoid.

Zac didn't have any clear answers for himself. He certainly wouldn't have any for Gibbs.

Anxious now to get back to his Wayward Ranch, Zac said, "This would seem to be pretty much wrapped up. If you thought you didn't need me or Trig anymore, we'd probably ride for the WO and then for home."

The Major thought for a long while before answering.

"Let's talk about it in the morning."

CHAPTER FORTY-TWO

When Zac emerged from the hotel the next morning his first stop was the jailhouse. Slim Gadfry was awake and angry. He had been shouting and making threats at the cowboy who was sitting in the office chair. The hollering became even louder when Zac walked in.

Zac walked over to the cell and said, "There was a day you'd have been hanging from a tree limb before now. You shut up and hold your peace. You're going to hang alright, but at least you'll get to wait until you hear a judge say the words. Now, not another sound out of you."

Zac walked over to the café for breakfast and found the whole group of riders from the livery loft were already there. Not seeing Pat, he turned and left. At the livery he found Pat frying up a couple of eggs on his little office stove. He had two pieces of bread spread out on a plate ready to receive the morning's fare.

"Morning, Pat. Thanks for letting those boys sleep in your loft. They may be here for a day or two. That's going to be up to the Major and the marshal, whenever he gets here.

"I'm thinking the Major will be wiring the lawman this morning, looking for directions."

"Already been done. I took care of it last evening. Tidy Walberg should be along right soon."

Recognizing that Pat was walking a narrow path of semi-secrecy, Zac simply nodded at the news. He rose, slapped Pat once on the shoulder and went in search of the Major. The two men met up in the hotel dining room.

Zac had no sooner taken his seat when Trig limped through the door. The Major waved him over.

"For a gunshot man you're up early, young fellow."

Trig nodded and took a seat. Pointing his thumb at Zac, he answered, "Tried leaving me behind the once. Just as likely to try it again. Figured I'd better get to looking after myself."

The Major smiled but remained quiet. Zac acted as if he had heard nothing. Johnny Gibbs held his normal, neutral façade.

Major Gantry smiled just a bit at Zac and Trig.

"As soon as the town office opens for business, we'll have to try to explain to someone why we arrested their sheriff and deputies and took over the jail."

After thinking this through for just a few seconds, and remembering the military way, Zac suggested, "We could volunteer Lucas. He's well known and respected. Probably the right man for the job."

The Major laughed in delight at the suggestion.

"And he's not here to object."

Trig looked around the table, studying the devious planners.

"I believe I'll have to be very careful around you men."

Even Johnny Gibbs laughed a bit.

Zac waited for the waitress to pour coffee before speaking.

"I'm guessing everyone sees you as heading this

thing up, Major. And I'm good with that too. But I'm just a bit concerned that there's only the one man holding down the sheriff's office. Might be better if he had a bit of help with all those prisoners."

The Major nodded his head in agreement and glanced at his foreman.

"Johnny, just as soon as you finish your meal will you take care of that please?"

Johnny Gibbs pushed his plate away and rose to his feet. Without a word he left the room. He returned in less that five minutes, saying nothing. He pulled his plate close again and continued eating as if nothing had been said or done.

Zac and Trig watched this interplay between the Major and the Lazee foreman. Neither said anything, but clearly, the Major's request had been received as an order to be carried out promptly.

When the breakfast was completed and the table cleared of everything but the coffee cups, Zac addressed the Major again, bringing up the talk from the night before.

"What do you see happening now, sir? I'm told the marshal has been informed and is on his way. I have no idea where he was or how long he will take to get here. And I don't know if there's a judge in town who can hear the case.

"Trig and I would kind of like to move on. Do you think we're needed now?"

The Major lit a cigar, his first of the day. It would be followed by exactly two others. No more. No less.

"Could you spare two more days? If the marshal is not here in that time, we'll have to think on what to do. In the meantime, there is still that wounded marshal out at the A-Bar. He knows the story on this end. But the rustling and murders on the WO and the butchering of cattle in the gold fields is your story to tell. It would be good to have you here."

CHAPTER FORTY-THREE

The next two days went by quietly and slowly. The men took full advantage of the rare opportunity for rest. By the Major's orders there was little drinking.

To bolster the evidence regarding the thefts and murders on the WO, Zac wired Santa Fe, asking that a message be immediately delivered to the ranch. The result was that only hours before the marshal and judge arrived, Claire, Anna and Leonard rode into Albuquerque. Walter was still not well enough to make the ride.

Mid morning, four days after Pat sent the wire, the marshal rode into town. He made no mention of where he had been. Riding beside him, and leading a heavily loaded pack animal, was a dusty, but well-dressed older man. Marshal Walberg introduced him to the Major and the others as Judge Reuben Claxton.

The judge was clearly a man of purpose and determination. Nor was he a man to waste time.

Immediately upon the completion of the introductions he took charge of the situation.

"I will be in my room at the hotel for exactly two hours. Marshal, you have that time to examine the prisoners and the evidence. The accused must be represented by an attorney, assuming one is available.

"Major, please use your authority to secure a suitable space for a trial. The saloon will do if no other can be found.

"I will tolerate no weapons in my courtroom, save for the marshal and whoever he appoints as deputies.

"And now, if a couple of you young men will assist in moving my goods to the hotel that would be greatly appreciated."

The judge turned and walked to the hotel, assuming that his orders would be followed. Two cowboys rolled up the oiled canvas tarpaulin covering the judge's pack and untied the paniers.

Exactly two hours later, Judge Claxton, bathed, shaved and in clean clothing walked out of the front door of the hotel. To anyone watching it was clear that, indeed, the judge was ready to hold court.

The tables in the saloon had been stacked into a far corner. The floor had been swept and fresh sawdust laid out. The chairs were neatly set into rows, with an aisle down the center. A large table was placed at the rear of the small room, near the back door. This would be used by the judge. A witness chair was located nearby.

The saloon was packed with witnesses and onlookers. The saloon owner and his two waiters were stationed behind the bar, mostly to prevent some eager cowboy from filching a bottle. They would also be where they were needed for serving drinks, immediately after the court abandoned the premises.

The judge was escorted through the rear door and took his seat. There was little chance of formality in the frontier setting. Judge Reuben Claxton simply banged the table three times with a small wooden mallet he had brought with him and shouted for all to hear.

"Court is in session."

There was a great shuffling of feet and sliding of chair legs as the late comers forced their way into the space. A glaring Judge Claxton soon put an end to the disturbance.

"Marshal, have you determined that you and your men are the only ones here with weapons available to them?"

Marshal Tidy Walberg stood. "I believe that to be correct, Your Honor."

"Bring in the prisoners."

There was a delay as the well-bound men shuffled across the street and into the court room. They were escorted to the chairs directly in front of the judge's desk.

When all was again in order the hammer hit the table just once. It was enough to gain everyone's attention.

"Are the defendants represented by legal counsel?"

An elderly man sitting close by the judge's table slowly rose.

"Your Honor, I have been invited, at the last minute, to speak for these men. My name, sir, is Wasp Tilbury, attorney at law, retired.

"I preferred to not take on this task. But it would appear that no other counsel in town was prepared to stand in for the accused. My last attendance in a courtroom was some years ago. But assuming that guilt and innocence still mean what those words have always portrayed, I will endeavor to see to as fair a trial as possible."

Judge Claxton merely nodded. He was scribbling something in a ledger. Wasp Tilbury, looking on, assumed the man was making note of his name.

Without raising his eyes from the ledger, the judge said, "Marshal, what are we dealing with here?"

"We're dealing with cattle rustling, horse theft and murder, your Honor."

"And my information is that a fellow deputy is one of the wounded. Is that correct, Marshal?"

"Yes, unfortunately. Bud Skaggett was wounded in the gun fight when the rustlers were captured. He apparently shows every sign of living through his injuries, but he was unable to travel, being under care and confined to bed at the A-Bar ranch."

A loud snort was heard throughout the courtroom, followed by, "layabout," spoken in an audible whisper.

Several eyes turned to Trig, wondering what the expression of disgust was all about. The judge chose not to hear the short interruption.

Judge Claxton lifted his head and leaned back in the saloon chair. He took a long study of Sheriff Slim Gadfry. After sorting out his thoughts, and with a voice echoing sadness, he spoke to this man he had known for years.

"Sheriff Gadfry, what do you have to say for yourself? If you are truly involved in this unfortunate mess you might just as well admit it now. There are witnesses enough. We will have the truth in the next hour in any case.

"If witnesses are lying and you are truly innocent of the charges, the court would be pleased to hear that now.

"Hearing the truth directly from you might go

some distance in restoring what little respect is left to your name."

Slim Gadfry, so defiant and angry when he was first arrested, found no words to respond to the question. With his eyes fixed firmly on the floor in front of him, he allowed the opportunity to speak pass by him.

The defence counsel had nothing to say.

The judge waited a considerable length of time before addressing the marshal again.

"Who do you have for witnesses, Marshal?"

"Sir, there are several people the court may wish to hear from. The first is Monty Abbot, one of the accused, and formerly a rider for the A-Bar. Mister Abbot has confessed his actions."

The judge wrote the name in his journal before motioning towards the witness chair.

"Your presence is required, Mister Abbot."

Before the prisoner could speak, Wasp Tilbury stood to his feet.

"Your honor, Mister Abbot has agreed to fully testify to this matter under an agreement for reasonable clemency, made with Mister Zac Trimbell. Mister Trimbell, as you may already know, was assisting Deputy Marshal Bud Skaggett in the arrest of the rustlers.

"It is my understanding that Marshal Walberg is in sympathy with this agreement."

The judge tapped his pencil on the tabletop while he thought this through. Finally, he asked, "And what authority did this Zac Trimbell have to make any kind of an agreement in a matter this serious?"

Marshal Walberg had remained standing during this exchange. He answered the judge's question.

"Your Honor, in these pioneer times, where law and order is often unofficial and commonly carried out without benefit of the courts, Mister Trimbell, in the midst of a gun fight where three men died and two were wounded, was attempting to bring a satisfactory conclusion to the thefts and murders on the WO and other ranches, without resorting to precipitate actions.

"Forcing an end to the gun battle that may have left the court without a living witness, Mister Trimbell was able to disarm and arrest Mister Abbot.

"Mister Trimbell's efforts towards solving the rustling had already led him and others on a long hunt ending in Georgetown, Colorado. He located the remains of the stolen cattle and drove them, with some assistance, back to the WO.

"The Georgetown sheriff was assisted by Mister Trimbell in the arrest and imprisonment of several men in and around Georgetown who were involved in the thefts.

"Those were the men who stood before you two weeks ago, Your Honor.

"The prisoners in this courtroom today are the remnants of a well-organized band of rustlers. Mister Monty Abbot was a part of that group. He has agreed to testify on condition that he receive favorable consideration in sentencing. And to answer your question directly, Mister Trimbell assumed no authority to himself. He merely assured the prisoner that he would speak to me about the matter. He has done that, and I concur with his offer to Mister Abbot."

Judge Claxton went through the motions of hearing from every witness, although he kept their stories to bare facts only.

Counsellor Tilbury was shown considerable latitude during the proceedings. But there was no doubt at all about what the outcome would be.

Judge Claxton addressed the court before sentencing was announced.

"I fear there is much more to this sordid tale than what we have heard in court today. The matter of where there is a market substantial enough to absorb so many animals will, seemingly remain a mystery.

"Since I am prepared to accept as fact, that it would take more men than those few before us to-day to carry out all the crimes we have heard of in this court, I regret to admit that some perpetrators will go free and unnamed.

"I commend the diligence and energy of those men and women, marshals and ranchers alike, who have worked to bring the rustling and murders to an end. Let us pray that the community is free of this type of activity, now and into the future."

When the gavel hit the desk a final time, signifying the end of the trial, Monty Abbot had been sentenced to five years in the penitentiary. Sheriff Slim Gadfry, Bobby Cromwell and Cal, the rider who tried to escape the A-Bar ranch yard, had all been sentenced to be hung.

Although there was great satisfaction that the rustling ring had been broken, there was no rejoicing or celebrating. The condemned men were all former friends and fellow cowboys on the Albuquerque area ranches.

The slow ride back to the A-Bar was solemn.

No one but the Major and his two riders chose to stay behind to see the sentences carried out.

Lucas Wishart begged off, admitting that to see his long-time friend and foreman hung was beyond his level of endurance.

Zac, Trig and the riders from the WO left town within an hour of the trial's end. They would camp out one night on the long ride back to the ranch.

CHAPTER FORTY-FOUR

Like the crew returning to the A-Bar and the J-J, the WO group were quiet, sitting around their dying fire. They had put some miles behind them, alternating between a ground covering trot and a slow lope.

Zac had again been fighting his inner thoughts, with deep depression following close behind.

During the long day's ride, he had allowed his gelding to drop a half mile behind the others. Leonard slowed, turning in the saddle to study the man, thinking to wait for him. Claire thought she understood what was on Leonard's mind.

"Leave him be."

Leonard turned to the front again and pushed his horse a bit to catch up with her. His eyes held an unasked question.

"Just let him be, Leonard. You don't know and you may never know. If you knew you'd not likely understand. Just let him be."

Trig and Anna couldn't help overhearing. Together they rode forward, with questions, but with no more said.

Although Zac's cavalry troupe had won some skirmishes all those years ago, they had lost even more.

And paid the heavy price.

Now, with the rustling matter put behind the ranchers and himself, he wasn't sure what they had truly won. If they could call it a win, it was a bitter win. Men, some good, others not so good, were dead. Others were injured. Even with the re-covered animals, the losses were great. Friendships had been broken. Trusts lost. Wasted weeks were spent riding the country during the search.

Ever demanding more of himself than he ex-pected of others, Zac wondered if he had done everything possible to bring the rustling and mur-ders to an end. Could he have saved lives by doing something differently?

He was attempting to sort this out in his mind when it all seemed to start running together, out of control, with no conscious thought.

The rustling, the slaughterhouse in George-town, the many cavalry attacks, the flaming cabin, the flat-topped mesa, the hidden canyons with the stolen herds, the screams of the dying, his little girl, crying, holding her hands out as if to say "Daddy, save me", the grave stones, the broken trusts, the question: 'Is it still well with your soul?'

The unbidden images, one on top of another, in no particular order, thundered through his mind. He seemed to have no strength to stop them.

Was he going crazy? Was he already crazy? Would the pain ever stop? And then the question. Always the question. 'Is it well with your soul?'

Well, is it? He hadn't truly asked himself that question for a long time.

He vaguely remembered the last black attack. Back there in the rustler's canyon, not many days before. He had wished he could remember how to pray.

As he often did, he gripped the saddle horn, closed his eyes and hung his head, trusting the gelding. The kaleidoscope of images was still there, although seemingly more distant than it was before.

He was left mentally and emotionally exhausted.

His sense of loss was almost overwhelming. It was as if his very soul was damaged and hurting. He could feel a dampness forming in the corners of his eyes.

Silently, but from the depth of his heart he said, "Lord?"

CHAPTER FORTY-FIVE

The riders pulled up at the turn-off to the WO. It wasn't necessary for them to ride all the way into Santa Fe. Cutting off to the northwest would save them many miles of travel. In spite of their efforts to encourage Zac and Trig to ride with them to the WO, Zac was determined to head directly to town and then to his Wayward Ranch.

Anna pushed her gelding close to Zac and laid her hand on top of his, resting on the horn.

"Walter will be disappointed. I know he'd want to thank you again and wish you well. Won't you reconsider?"

"I've been thanked. By Walter and by all of you. Trig can make his own decision, but my wish is to get back to my own ranch. We're not all that far apart. It's possible we'll run into each other again some day.

"You wish Walter a fast healing for me. If I was any help at all, you need to know I'm pleased to have been asked. But now, I'll keep riding home."

Anna thanked him again before Claire rode over and touched his arm.

"You're a very special man, Zac Trimbell. And don't you ever doubt that. I will carry my gratitude all my days. I pray God will see you through."

With that she stood in her stirrups and gave him a quick kiss on the cheek.

Both women then converged on Trig. Anna spoke first.

"Trig, what Claire just said about Zac is equally true of you. You are a very special man. Without the two of you Walter and I would be dead and the WO ranch would be valueless. I can say no more. If we talked here for the next hour all I would do is repeat my thanks. God bless you. I hope you understand that if there is ever a need we are here."

Trig, ever ready with a thought to ease the tension said, "Don't forget that black and white dog of yours. He's the one that found you."

Again, Trig was grinning from ear to ear, while the others laughed.

Leonard shook hands with both departing men. No words were spoken or needed.

A few minutes later, as the two groups were riding apart, Claire pulled her horse to a stop and turned in the saddle. Neither Zac nor Trig were looking back. Trig had turned once just moments before, but she hadn't seen that.

The two men rode in silence, each with their own thoughts.

Finally, Zac broke the stillness between them.

"I thought you were planning to go back to the WO. Seems to me you had the hand of a certain woman on your mind."

Trig pushed his hat back in some kind of a signal, and grinned.

"Why, shucks. Didn't you take note of how those two were studying on each other? Me butting in on that put me in mind of trying to climb one of those higher flat-topped mesas. That small one we went up was enough for me.

"As to ladies, seems to me there might be more hopeful challenges. Down the road somewhere, is what I mean to say."

Zac responded with one of his rare smiles.

They kicked their horses into a faster lope and headed for Santa Fe.

Zac and Trig loafed around Santa Fe for two days. They both took advantage of the opportunity for a bath, a haircut and hotel rooms. They found a trading post and purchased new clothing.

Zac studied the torn knee on his canvas pants.

"Don't know if I should bother having this washed and mended or not.

Trig laughed.

"Why, partner, them pants were wore out before you ever got caught up in this little adventure."

Zac looked at the pants once more.

"I suppose you're right on that. Might just as well throw this shirt away at the same time."

On their second day in town, bathed and fixed up in their new clothing, Zac and Trig went looking for Martin Garcia. When he wasn't in his sheriff's office, they strolled over to the little cantina they had found him in on the ride south. He was sitting over his mid day lunch.

Without an invitation, the two men pulled out chairs and sat down.

Martin studied them for just a moment before asking, "Why don't you fellas have a seat. Join me?"

Zac got right to the matter that had been troubling him.

"Martin, I've always thought highly of you. We've done a bit of work together, you and me. It was you that sent Miss Maddison to the Wayward looking for help.

"When we were here a short while ago, we asked you about the southern ranches. The ones that had reported rustled herds."

The sheriff laid down his fork. "A-Bar, J-J, Lazee. If I don't misremember."

"That's the ones. We, that's Trig here, and me, we rode down there. It took a bit of digging around, but we found the cattle and the thieves. At least some of them. Found a couple of surprises too.

"The other thing that surprised me, Martin, was your reaction when we were here doing the asking. At the mention of the ranches, you left the table, offering no explanation. But bringing our conversation to such a sudden close left me with a couple of unanswered questions. How about you think back and answer those questions now."

"Not sure I know exactly what question you might have had."

"Sure, you do, Martin. We've only known each other for a couple of years but you have a good reputation as sheriff. And I've never known you to shy from a challenge. Never known you to be scared. But you were scared that day."

Martin picked up his fork and ate another bite of lunch. The waitress came and offered coffee to Zac and Trig. With a simple nod from Trig, she poured the cups full and quietly walked away.

Zac gave his old friend time to sort out his answer.

Martin pushed the nearly empty plate away. He looked at the two men sitting across from him and knew they weren't going to quit without an answer.

"Hard to say this, boys. I'd rather lie to you, but you'd see through the lie. The fact is, I was scared. I'm still just a bit scared, not knowing all that's happened down south.

"There's some hard men involved in that whole mess. I only know who a couple of them are but that's enough. I knew I could never stand before them by myself. I'm not a coward. At least I never have been before. Someone comes at me with a gun or a knife or his fists, I'll not be running away.

"But I'll admit those boys scared me. The two of them came right into my office and left me with a warning. Threatened my wife with vile things. I knew they wouldn't be offering no fair fight. Yes, they scared me.

"You have to understand that my job is here in Santa Fe. I'm not a county sheriff or marshal. The warning I got was to just stick to my own job and not to get involved in anything else. I did that for a time.

"But when the WO was hit, I had to do whatever I could. Walter and Anna are good people. Friends of mine. So, I went out there when Anna's sister came to me. Right away I could see that most of the herd was gone. The two murdered cowboys put a cap on the whole thing. The rustlers were meaning business.

"That's when I told Anna's sister to ride to Las Vegas and find you, Zac. I couldn't leave on a hunt and still keep this job. She needed someone who was free to travel. Someone the thieves wouldn't know on sight.

"Anyway, I don't know of anyone more willing or able to help folks than you, Zac. It's almost like it's your calling in life."

That short speech left the table in silence for a full minute.

Trig set his coffee mug down and broke the silence.

"Can you give us some names? Like of the couple of men you said frightened you the most."

"Major Gantry's name strikes fear everywhere it's spread. A hard man. Hard crew. Seems he's not in on the rustling but I was warned that if I didn't stay out of it, the word would be passed to the Major that I was one of the leaders of the rustlers. I didn't figure the Major would give me much of an opportunity to explain."

"Who else?"

"Slim Gadfry. Sheriff in Albuquerque. Another hard man. Don't care who he hurts. Up to his neck in the business.

"Just those two were enough to keep me in town. Until they hit the WO, as I just told you."

Zac wondered how to proceed. He had the feeling there was more. Perhaps it was time to tell a bit of what happened down to the south.

"You don't have to worry about either of those men. I know the Major from the war. We were posted together for a time. He's firm but fair. And Slim Gadfry isn't sheriff anymore. In fact, the court sentenced him to be hung. We left town before that was done but I expect it's over by this time."

Martin showed sudden relief on his face.

Zac still wasn't satisfied.

"I'm thinking you might still be holding something back. I'm having trouble believing that you were so easily set aside."

Martin smiled just a bit, spreading his hands before him, on the table, and dropping his voice even lower than it had been.

"Just between us, boys?"

Zac and Trig both nodded their assent.

"I called the federal marshals into the thing. I figured if I couldn't do the job perhaps it was best to bring in someone that could."

Zac leaned back in his chair, smiling. Trig slapped the table with his hand and then reached over and slapped Martin on the shoulder.

CHAPTER FORTY-SIX

The next morning, Zac saddled up to head home. Back to his Wayward Ranch. Trig, with his horse stalled next to Zac's gelding, was carefully adjusting his saddle.

Zac watched him for a while before saying, "I always seem to be wondering what you're up to. Still don't know. I'm riding home. Where are you headed?"

Trig smiled over the back of his horse.

"I ain't had so much fun since us kids used to go skinny dipping, back in the piney woods swamps, while leaving Emma-May Kratz on the bank to warn of water moccasins, on account of she was too shy to take off her flour sack dress, and join us in the water.

"I figure to follow along if'n that don't upset you too much. I've still got a few coins in my pocket. I don't mind covering off the cost of grub and coffee. Of course, I'd enjoy the whole thing just as much if there was some way to prevent gett'n shot again."

Zac figured if he shook his head any more at this young man, he just might shake it loose.

The ride from Santa Fe to Las Vegas could be covered in one long day but there was no need of that. The two travellers made a comfortable camp along a small creek, turning the long ride into two short ones.

Zac was still quiet during the ride, easing out of his latest battle with depression and mental horror. Trig was wise enough to leave him to his own thoughts.

Arriving in Las Vegas, Zac went first to the sheriff's office to say hello to his friend. Link Spangler greeted him from the curved-back chair placed comfortably in the shade on the board walk.

"Zac. Climb down there and come so's I can shake your hand. The news is that you not only broke up the rustler ring but that you saved the fair maiden in the process."

Zac shook Link's hand and sat in the second chair.

"I hardly think that accurately describes things, but we'll let it go. What makes me wonder though is how the word got here before I did."

Link laughed at the remark.

"Are you forgetting about the telegraph? There's just no secrets anymore. And by the way, there's a wire waiting for you over at the depot. Who is this riding with you?"

"Link, I'd like you to say hello to Trig Mason. He's ridden all the same trails I rode these past weeks. Good man hunting tracks. Don't much like being shot though."

The two men shook hands. Link said, "Been shot a time or two my own self. I don't recommend it."

After the three men shared all the news, Zac and Trig mounted up again.

"Don't forget to pick up that wire."

Zac re-mounted outside the depot and nudged the gelding into a slow walk while he tore the envelope open. He read the wire and then read it again.

"Well, ain't that something!"

He smiled and passed the wire to Trig.

"Coming west. Stop. Confirm current location. Stop." Rev. Moody Tomlinson.

Zac took the wire back from Trig.

"Wait here just a few minutes. I'll go answer this."

A LOOK AT: MAC'S WAY

Raised in poverty in Missouri, Mac is determined to find a better life for himself and the girl who is still a vague vision in his mind. Work on the Santa Fe Trail, and on a Mississippi River boat give him a start, but the years of Civil War leave him broke and footloose in South Texas. There he discovers more cattle running loose than he ever knew existed. Teaming up with two ex-Federal soldiers, he sets out to gather his wealth, one head at a time.

While gathering and driving Longhorns, Mac and his friends meet an interesting collection of characters, including Margo. Mac and Margo and the crew learn about Longhorns, and life, from hard experience before they eventually head west. Outlaws and harrowing river crossings are just two of the challenges they face along their way.

AVAILABLE NOW ON AMAZON FROM REG QUIST AND CKN CHRISTIAN PUBLISHING

ABOUT THE AUTHOR

Reg Quist's pioneer heritage includes sod shacks, prairie fires, home births, and children's graves under the prairie sod, all working together in the lives of people creating their own space in a new land.

Out of that early generation came farmers, ranchers, business men and women, builders, military graves in faraway lands, Sunday Schools that grew to become churches, plus story tellers, musicians, and much more.

Quist's writing career was late in pushing itself forward, remaining a hobby while family and career took precedence. Only in early retirement, was there time for more serious writing.

Woven through every story is the thought that, even though he was not there himself in that pioneer time, he knew some that were. They are remembered with great respect.

Find more great titles by Reg Quist and Christian Kindle News at http://christiankindlenews.com/our-authors/reg-quist/